THEY WERE FROM DIFFERENT WORLDS.

Perhaps even different centuries.

His gaze locked on her upturned face. "You upset me in ways no other woman ever has."

"Clay?" she whispered.

He knew he was behaving with uncharacteristic recklessness as he leaned closer, but he couldn't control the impulses seething within his body. He claimed the promise of her lips in the next heartbeat.

She tasted of sweetness and comfort and salvation. She tasted of other things as well, things that shocked him—Welcome and desire.

Pleasure lanced through him, then rocked him right down to the soles of his feet.

She gripped his narrow waist, her lips parting even more as she angled her head. "Yes. Oh, yes," she breathed against his mouth.

Had he imagined her words? he wondered. Or had he simply heard the echo of his own desire?

As if sensing his hesitation, Kelly deepened their kiss.

WHAT ARE *LOVESWEPT* ROMANCES?

They are stories of true romance and touching emotion. We believe those two very important ingredients are constants in our highly sensual and very believable stories in the LOVESWEPT line. Our goal is to give you, the reader, stories of consistently high quality that may sometimes make you laugh, sometimes make you cry, but are always fresh and creative and contain many delightful surprises within their pages.

Most romance fans read an enormous number of books. Those they truly love, they keep. Others may be traded with friends and soon forgotten. We hope that each LOVESWEPT romance will be a treasure—a "keeper." We will always try to publish

LOVE STORIES YOU'LL NEVER FORGET
BY AUTHORS YOU'LL ALWAYS REMEMBER

The Editors

Loveswept ® 822

CLOUD DANCER

LAURA TAYLOR

BANTAM BOOKS
NEW YORK · TORONTO · LONDON · SYDNEY · AUCKLAND

CLOUD DANCER

A Bantam Book / February 1997

*LOVESWEPT and the wave design are registered trademarks of
Bantam Books, a division of Bantam Doubleday Dell Publishing Group,
Inc. Registered in U.S. Patent and Trademark Office and elsewhere.*

ISBN 0-553-44560-X

Published simultaneously in the United States and Canada

*Bantam Books are published by Bantam Books, a division of Bantam Dou-
bleday Dell Publishing Group, Inc. Its trademark, consisting of the words
"Bantam Books" and the portrayal of a rooster, is Registered in U.S. Patent
and Trademark Office and in other countries. Marca Registrada. Bantam
Books, 1540 Broadway, New York, New York 10036.*

PRINTED IN THE UNITED STATES OF AMERICA

OPM   0 9 8 7 6 5 4 3 2 1

This book is dedicated to
Marc and Alanna Almgren
as they begin their life together
as husband and wife.
I wish you great happiness, my
friends.

Dear Reader,

I am delighted to have been invited to participate in the *Treasured Tales* month of books for Loveswept. This invitation provided me with an opportunity to share with you in *Cloud Dancer* my admiration and respect for the rich cultural traditions of the many Native American Indian tribes that I learned about as I conceived and developed this story.

I would also like you to know that this book would not have been possible without the enthusiastic support of my editor at Bantam, Beth de Guzman, and her assistant, Cassie Goddard. As well, I depended on fellow author, friend, and history buff Bruce Stine for a grasp of the events surrounding the November 1864 massacre at Sand Creek, in Colorado. Allowing for the literary license needed during the writing of a fictional story, any errors are, of course, mine to claim.

Cloud Dancer is the Cheyenne name of a sophisticated, Harvard-educated man from another century. Transplanted into the white world during adolescence and given the name Clay Sloan, he is a unique product of two very diverse cultures.

I think you can imagine the potential conflicts and challenges inherent in this situation, especially if you combine them, as I decided to do, with a tragic event based in historical fact that results in his being transported more than a hundred and thirty-five years forward in time.

Are you intrigued by the possibilities? I hope so, because I certainly was, especially when viewed from the perspective of Kelly Farrell, who has her orderly little world turned upside down by our very unusual and seductive hero.

The chemistry between Kelly and Clay fascinated me as I wrote this book—perhaps because they seemed, and still seem, quite real to me. Allied against the unknown, this hero and heroine have reminded me that love transcends all our pragmatic perceptions of time and place. I hope they will give you the same gift as you read Kelly and Clay's story.

Cloud Dancer is my fifteenth book for Loveswept, and I thank you for your support and encouraging letters as each one has been published.

Laura Taylor

ONE

The Past . . .

The thirty-six-year-old man known among the Cheyenne as Cloud Dancer felt the exuberance of his lost youth as he rode the Colorado back country. He savored the clean air, towering fir trees, and multicolored wildflowers that carpeted the rugged terrain.

Soon he would be with his people in the village of his boyhood. Clad in beaded elkskins and moccasins, he'd already shed the garments that symbolized the constraints of the life he'd lived for so many years. It would take longer to shed the influence of that life, but he felt confident he could.

He sensed that his heart was on the brink of breaking free of his body and gliding like an eagle above the mountain peaks. He smiled then, the enigmatic image he'd always presented to the world notably absent.

He wondered what the people of Boston and Washington would think if they saw him now. They knew him as a loner, an attorney with a gift for oratory, and as the adopted son of a socially prominent New England banker.

His mother, the only child of a Cheyenne holy man, and his stepfather were dead. As their sole heir, he'd settled their estate and invested the considerable assets left to him for later use on behalf of his people.

He'd learned the ways of the whites, as much to aid his mother in her adjustment to her new life as to show respect for the stepfather who adopted him, gave him his name, and loved him like a son. Along the way he'd also learned to navigate the ignorance and curiosity of Boston high society; in effect, to set himself apart from it. Most people considered him a barely tamed savage, especially the fathers and suitors of the sophisticated daughters of established families.

Unable to conceal their fascination, the debutantes had amused him over the years. The adventurous among them had invited him into their beds. He'd accepted their attentions without ever giving his heart. His culture bred a man to claim what he needed in order to survive in an unforgiving land, and he never allowed himself to forget that philosophy.

He openly celebrated his heritage, taking

pride in it and using it to sustain himself when loneliness ravaged his soul.

Cloud Dancer's smile broadened. Anticipation and eagerness prompted him to push his mount even harder in the minutes that followed. His twenty-year absence was almost at an end. As it had many times before, his shaman grandfather's voice echoed in his thoughts: "You may not be with us in body, but your spirit remains lodged with The People. You will return to us when the time is right. Be brave, young warrior, for you will be tested."

The man known as Clayton Sloan Jr. in the white world guided his horse up the steepening incline. He already knew what he would see when he reached the plateau atop the hill and gazed across the valley—a village humming with life.

The women would be preparing food and overseeing their children. Innocent maidens would be giggling as they inspected their marriage prospects. Young boys eager for manhood would be caring for horses and indulging in fantasies of counting coups, while seasoned warriors supervised their activities, sharpened their weapons, and told embellished tales of triumphant encounters over old enemies.

A wolf howled in the distance, startling him and making his horse skittish. The sound struck him as odd. It was a sound he associated with the night, not of a sun-washed summer morning in the Colorado mountains. He knew that the wolf frightened many with its powerful medicine, but the animal had never stirred fear in his heart. It reminded him of his people and their respect for all the creatures given breath by the Great Spirit.

He recalled then the lone wolf that had wailed mournfully throughout the night following the death of his father. Coming on the heels of his ninth birthday, the loss of his father had left a wound in his heart that no one, not even his wise and loving stepfather, had had the power to heal.

Cloud Dancer frowned when he spotted the billowing brown clouds that marred the azure morning sky just seconds before he topped the hill. He reined in his horse, then slid off the winded animal. Suddenly anxious about what awaited his gaze if he looked down across the valley, he studied the expanding dark clouds.

Carried aloft by the gusting breezes, the scent of smoke mingled with the telltale stench of death. He recoiled, then calmed himself by the sheer force of his will.

The birds had disappeared, their songs absent. Dogs no longer barked. There were no voices. There was no laughter. The deafening sound of silence persisted, save for the cawing of the buzzards swooping through the sky before they settled on the high branches of the trees below.

He made himself lower his gaze, made himself study the valley. His heart stopped beating. The devastation he saw stunned him, rendering him still with shock. He refused to believe his eyes at first, but the cruel reality of the massacre failed to disappear as he blinked and then re-focused on what remained of the village.

An anguish-filled cry of denial emerged from his soul and burst out of him. It echoed across the landscape, eventually returning to ram into his consciousness like a fist slamming into his chest. Gasping, he fell to his knees, his despair so great that he felt momentarily paralyzed. He scanned the scene below, praying he was imagining the bodies strewn about like discarded rag dolls.

Pushing himself up from his kneeling posi-tion, he raced down the hillside, falling more than once, bloodying his hands on exposed rocks as he righted himself and scratching his face on low tree branches. He was beyond feeling or car-ing or even noticing the pain.

As he stumbled through the ruined village and among the fallen bodies, he moaned. A Cheyenne death chant summoned from memory passed his lips. The slaughter had been whole-sale, hundreds of lives ended by well-aimed bul-lets and mutilating knife wounds within the last hour. Probably during a pre-dawn raid.

He saw, too, the terror and shock etched into the faces of the victims. The life-force still seeped from the women, children, and warriors, merging to form blackening pools that soaked the soil. Some tepees smoldered. Others burned like torches, the wind carrying the flames to those few structures missed by the raiders.

"Why?" he shouted over and over again. "Why?"

Cloud Dancer continued to walk among the dead, too sick at heart to think with the clarity he usually possessed. Tears trailed down his hard cheeks. He wept openly as he searched for survivors. There were none.

He cared little that his emotions were so obvious or that some would consider them womanly. There was no one left to witness his weakness. His head pounded with a combination of rage and pain unlike anything he'd ever experienced. Vows of revenge spilled out of him in Cheyenne.

His grief mounted, encompassing him like a black mist when he discovered his grandfather's body at the entrance to the burning medicine lodge. He knelt beside the elderly holy man, his hands shaking as he closed the sightless eyes and reverently traced the weathered contours of his face.

Huddled over the lifeless form, he sobbed. Cloud Dancer's dream of reclaiming his honor and his place among the Cheyenne died in that instant. He knew what he must do.

Gathering the desecrated body of the legendary shaman into his arms, he shoved himself to his feet, paused to give voice to a prayer to the Great Spirit, then walked into the welcoming embrace of the flames that would end his anguish once and for all.

The Present . . .

Sprawled on his back, Cloud Dancer floundered in the thick mist that shrouded his mind and body. His muscles quivered like taut piano wire as he struggled for control over them, and his throat was so parched that it hurt each time he swallowed.

His return to consciousness happened in stages. Every time he dragged in enough air to feed his starving lungs, he choked on the smoke and ash he inhaled. The sensation that he was on the verge of suffocating spurred him to orient himself to his surroundings.

Cloud Dancer fought for every breath he took in the moments that followed, instinct rather than lucid thought guiding his struggle for survival. Demons suddenly screamed, shattering the silence with sounds so alien to him that his entire body stiffened with shock. His heart thundered in his chest. His pulse raced.

Cloud Dancer opened his eyes, but he saw nothing other than the dense smoke of the spirit world. His anxiety escalating, it took him a moment to realize this was death—a death he'd willingly sought upon discovering that his quest for forgiveness and redemption had become little more than a funeral pyre for his dreams and his people.

He groaned, tears of regret seeping from his burning, red-rimmed eyes. Anguish flooded his soul as nightmarish images of his massacred village pushed to the forefront of his mind.

He recalled then the ease with which he'd decided to join his people in death. The carnage he'd discovered had devastated him, the thought of living quickly losing all meaning for him. His hope for the future as lifeless as the grandfather he'd longed to see for so many years, he'd carried the shaman's body into the burning medicine lodge for the journey to the spirit world.

Demons wailed yet again, the sound chilling his soul. The serenity he'd expected in the afterlife was conspicuously absent.

Cloud Dancer curled his powerfully constructed body into a fetal position, covered his face with his hands, and breathed shallowly. He prayed for courage, then vowed he would face the Great Spirit with the strength of the youthful Cheyenne warrior he'd once been. His pride, the same pride that had helped him weather the disdain of the less tolerant of the white world for nearly twenty years, fueled his determination.

The demons continued to scream, seemingly intent on destroying his search for inner courage, but another sound, this one subtle but still discernible, nibbled at his awareness.

He concentrated, finally hearing a frail female

voice speak in the language he'd learned from his stepfather as an adolescent. "Please help me."

Shocked, Cloud Dancer didn't move. His thoughts scattered like fallen leaves pummeled by a fierce wind. Sanity and reason slowly re-emerged while he grappled with his surprise. He knew in his heart that the spirit world was not a place for whites; it was the world reserved for The People after death.

"Please," the weak voice entreated.

Cloud Dancer tried to ignore the plea for help, but it was like trying to ignore the still-shrieking demons or his urge to flee this hellish spirit world. Impossible.

Convinced that the Great Spirit had denied him entry to the afterlife of the Cheyenne as punishment for turning his back on his people for so many years, he shed bitter tears and groaned out an inarticulate protest.

He finally managed to regain his self-control.

The smoke grew thicker, blanketing him like a heavy tarp. Cloud Dancer repeatedly coughed as he tried to find a pocket of untainted air. Peering through the heavy smoke, he spotted flames shooting up through the plank floor, devouring it like a hungry beast and threatening to devour him as well.

"Help," she whispered again, her voice even more fragile.

A man of conscience, the same man who had set out on a mission to reclaim his honor as a warrior of the Cheyenne Nation, Cloud Dancer responded to the woman. He began to crawl in her direction, her moans guiding him through the smoke despite the strange heaviness of his limbs and the pain streaking like heat lightning through the muscles of his large, raw-boned body.

When he bumped against her slack form a few moments later, he struggled to his knees, drew her small body into his arms, and staggered to his feet. Cloud Dancer moved blindly through the smoke-engulfed building, stumbling when he slammed his shoulder against a doorframe and almost falling a second time as he tripped over a piece of furniture.

He cradled the semiconscious woman against his chest and protected her as best he could from the flames dancing along the walls on either side of them. At the end of what resembled a long tunnel, blurred lights beckoned.

Cloud Dancer hoped he'd found an escape route from the hell that surrounded them. Heat, flames, and gushing smoke pursued them as he crashed through a door and burst out of the building.

Again the demons wailed, closer this time and like an angry chorus. Although unnerved by the fierce sound and flashing lights all around him, survival dominated Cloud Dancer's thoughts. Still clutching the woman, he raced across a shallow porch, down a short flight of stairs, and into the night.

Gasping for air, he dropped to his knees as the roof of the building he'd just exited collapsed. Ash and sparks of flame exploded into the air and rode the gusting breeze, raining down upon the surrounding terrain.

Cloud Dancer placed the choking woman on the ground, then straightened and threw back his head. His broad chest heaving, he greedily drank in the cleansing night air. His hair cascaded across his shoulders and down past the center of his back like a midnight waterfall. His clothing, singed in spots, bloodstained and soot-covered, emphasized his harshly carved features and powerful physique.

Cloud Dancer was not a handsome man by any standards. He looked like what he was—a Cheyenne warrior educated but not completely civilized by the rarefied world into which he'd been adopted as an adolescent.

He briefly closed his eyes, fighting his rising panic as the ominous sounds and flashing lights of the spirit world hammered at his senses. When he reopened them and focused on his surroundings, he experienced even greater disorientation, thanks to the activity around him.

Enormous red machines rumbled into the yard, reminding him of locomotives he'd ridden in the east. Despite his confusion, he noticed they needed no iron tracks. People clothed in strange garments leapt from these machines that made piercing blasts of sound interspersed with low growls and dragged long, snakelike tubes from them. When water gushed with great force from the tubes, his mind produced an image of the fire brigades of Boston. He couldn't, however, ever remember viewing a fire scene like this one.

Suddenly aware of movement behind him, he turned his head and peered at the oddly attired and masked creature running toward him. His heart leapt into a hard gallop, but he held his position on his knees beside the old woman.

"Martha, are you all right?" The voice was female, as was the body visible below the neck, despite the bulky clothing. "Martha!"

Cloud Dancer succumbed to the impulse to distance himself from everything and everyone, not just this creature. Once the target of an angry mob, he knew better than to linger without a weapon among those who were not like him. He surged to his feet, the muscles of his body protesting the sudden movement as he headed across the yard.

Leaping over a white picket fence, he sought the protection and anonymity of darkness. He didn't pause to consider what awaited him in this unknown world. He simply prayed that the Great Spirit hadn't completely abandoned him and would guide his footsteps in this hellish afterlife.

"Wait! Please wait!" cried the demon. "Who are you?"

"I am Cloud Dancer," he answered eventually, although he knew no one would hear his words as he ran through a newly tilled farm field. "I am a warrior of the Cheyenne Nation, and I will never forget those who have been sacrificed on the altar of ignorance and greed."

He lost track of time as he traveled deeper into the back country, surrendering instead to the need to find a quiet place. Transcending the pain of exertion, his body shifted into a state of endurance reminiscent of boyhood contests that tested the physical and mental fitness of a prospective warrior. Once he reached a level of fatigue that assured him he would harm himself if he continued running, he spied the outbuildings, barn, and corral of a small ranch.

The horses in the barn nickered softly, as though to welcome a weary wanderer. An experienced horseman, Cloud Dancer found comfort in the familiar sounds and smells of the beautifully bred animals lodged in the stalls. He felt safe there, too, although he didn't understand why.

Too exhausted to formulate a better plan at that moment, Cloud Dancer fashioned a pallet in the clean hay, collapsed atop it, and fell into an exhausted slumber. He didn't dream. He slept the sleep of a man too exhausted to do anything else, a man who didn't realize he'd journeyed more than a hundred and thirty years through time.

TWO

Ten-year-old Joey Farrell disliked morning chores, but he did them because he was the man of the house. He reminded himself of that fact as he tugged open the barn door to check on the horses that July morning.

Making his way through the barn, he surveyed the grain supply and the water level in the low tubs in each horse stall. He walked slowly, an accomplishment for a boy of his age.

Taught from early childhood to respect the high-strung nature of the animals he dealt with, Joey rarely forgot that particular lesson. He also knew that the horses entrusted to his mother for lodging and training by their wealthy owners represented the income that sustained the ranch. He loved the ranch. It was his legacy, not just his home.

His thoughts drifting to the first day of summer camp, Joey almost missed the moccasined feet partially covered with hay in the final stall. Pausing, he glanced over his shoulder just to make sure his eyes weren't playing tricks on him. What he saw thrilled him even more than the prospect of leaving for sleep-away camp with his cousins later that morning.

Brown eyes huge with curiosity, Joey crept along the front edge of the stall's metal gate to get a better view. Holding his breath, he peered through the bars and studied the sleeping man stretched out on his side against the far wall of Bountiful's stall.

His amazement growing with every passing second, Joey debated his options. He took off like a launched rocket a few moments later. Racing out of the barn and across the yard, he jerked open the kitchen screen door and came to a skidding halt next to his mother.

Clad in jeans, a cropped cotton tee, and Western-style boots, Kelly Farrell stood in front of the stove. As she stirred scrambled eggs with a wooden spoon, she sipped her first cup of coffee of the day.

"Mom, there's a man in our barn!"

Kelly smiled tiredly at her son. She knew she should chastise him for telling tales, but his imagination, which generally worked overtime, was part of his personality. Like his late father, he loved making up stories, the more adventurous or outlandish the better.

"Really? What's his name?"

Jumping up and down with excitement, he exclaimed, "Mom! How would I know his name? I just found him."

"Maybe you should ask," she suggested, feeling whimsical enough to play his game. "It's the polite thing to do."

"Listen, Mom. You're not gonna believe this guy. He's really neat-looking."

"What's he doing?"

"Sleeping!" Joey hooted with laughter. "Isn't that great?" He sobered briefly. "Do you think he might be a 'scaped criminal? Wouldn't that be something?"

Kelly's smile widened. She couldn't help herself. Her fatigue invariably disappeared when Joey was nearby, even after a night that had dragged on until dawn. A volunteer firefighter in her rural Colorado community, she'd been part of the team that had responded to the blaze that had destroyed Martha Hurley's home and nearly taken her life. Hospitalized now, the elderly woman was expected to recover from her ordeal.

She could rest later, Kelly reminded herself as she glanced at her son. "He's sleeping, is he? I envy him."

Joey vibrated with barely suppressed energy. "Yeah. You gotta see him."

"Sweetie, your breakfast is almost ready." She turned off the gas flame beneath the pan. "Why don't you eat first? Your Aunt Kate will be here in about an hour."

"Aw, Mom, please. I'm not kidding around, I promise."

Kelly studied the expressive dark eyes and angular face so reminiscent of James Farrell. Her gaze then lingered on the silky black hair that crowned Joey's head and skimmed the collar of his shirt. He hated having it cut. She let him have his way about his hair during the summer months, because he insisted it made him feel closer to his father's people. Joey understood there was a price to pay when your mother was the principal of your grade school.

"Please," he begged. "This is for real."

Kelly covered the scrambled eggs with the lid of the frying pan, rinsed her hands at the sink, and dried them. "You're sure about that?"

"Hurry, Mom! He might leave."

"I'm hurrying," she said, her thoughts on the most recent addition to her stable as she followed him out the kitchen door and across the yard. "Was Bountiful any calmer this morning?"

"She's fine. I think she likes the guy."

Kelly's smile disappeared. She ran the rest of the way to the barn. Bountiful had been hell on wheels since her arrival earlier in the week, and she didn't need anything or anyone disturbing her.

Kelly stumbled to a stop the instant she got a good look at the sprawled body of the man in the stall with Bountiful, the filly sent to her for training by a Denver horse breeder unable to cope with the spirited animal. It took her a minute to realize that Bountiful had never seemed more at ease.

"Mom . . . ," Joey began.

Even though he whispered, Kelly clapped a hand over his mouth and shook her head. She needed . . . she didn't know what she needed, she realized as her gaze darted between Bountiful and the man sleeping within a few inches of Bountiful's hooved feet.

He suddenly rolled onto his back—all six feet and a couple of inches of buckskin-clad man. In response, Bountiful took a few mincing steps to one side but remained calm.

The man's attire gave Kelly pause. The intricate beading on his shirt and moccasins reminded her of garments preserved and displayed in a Denver museum she'd visited while still in college. Other than a few of the elders who sat on the Tribal Council, most local Cheyenne normally reserved their native clothing for ceremonial events. James had worn his great-grandfather's on their wedding day, but only because she'd asked him to humor her love of his tribal traditions.

Kelly edged closer, aware that Bountiful's companion might awaken at any moment. She noticed the soot that streaked his buckskin pants and shirt. She noticed, too, the scratches that marred his hands and face. She recognized him as the man who'd rescued Martha Hurley from her fire-ravaged home the previous night before sprinting off into the dark. She still didn't understand why he'd fled the scene after saving Martha from certain death, but that was the least of her problems at the moment.

Joey peeled her hand away from the lower half of his face. "What are we gonna do with him?" he whispered.

Kelly knew his real question was, *Can we keep him?* She peered down at Joey, pondering how to answer him. She didn't want her son treating a possible vagrant like a candidate for show-and-tell at school.

This man—whoever he was—clearly wasn't a potential adoptee, either, despite Joey's propensity for collecting strays. The latter was the last thing she needed, especially since she'd fired their hired man a few weeks earlier, and it was just the two of them living on the ranch until she could find someone new to help with the chores and the horses. She couldn't employ just anyone. She needed an experienced horseman, and they were as rare as hen's teeth at the wages she was able to offer.

"Do you think he's a criminal?" he asked, sounding hopeful.

"I think he's tired and hurt, Joey," she said softly.

The boy nodded. "Looks like he was in a fire, doesn't it, Mom?"

"Yes, it does."

Her gaze shifted to the man's exposed fore-arms, which were scorched an angry red. She saw no sign of blistering there, but she knew from experience that if he had any burn blisters, they could produce infections if not properly cared for. She wondered if he had any other injuries that needed immediate attention, then jumped when he stirred with a groan.

Something inside her responded to the low sound—the woman part, she realized. The part of herself she'd managed to ignore since the death of her husband six and a half years ago. Baffled by her strong reaction to him, she took a calming breath, shot a warning glance at her son, and let her gaze slide between Bountiful and her companion.

The man jerked in his sleep. He groaned once more, the emotional distress in the sound so pro-found that she felt his pain, even though she didn't have a clue as to the source of it. Bountiful whinnied softly, her response faintly sympathetic.

Relieved that the filly wasn't becoming agi-tated, Kelly inched backward as the man stirred. She drew Joey along with her. She needed to figure out how to handle this situation before he awakened.

The man's eyes snapped open, his gaze fixed on the high rafters of the barn. He exhaled, then coughed when he tried to drag fresh air into his lungs.

Kelly froze. The man coughed a second time. She concluded he was suffering from a mild case of smoke inhalation. Not surprising, since he'd apparently gone into a fully engulfed dwelling to rescue its sole occupant.

Bountiful nickered, moved to a spot near the man's shoulder, and, much to Kelly's amazement, nudged him ever so gently with her nose, as though expressing compassion. It was a fanciful thought, but Kelly believed in the compassionate nature of animals. Often, she had found, they were kinder than humans.

The man lifted his hand, then absently stroked the animal's long nose as he slowly inhaled and exhaled.

Kelly held her breath, waiting for Bountiful to lose her famous temper. Surprisingly, she didn't.

Bountiful nickered again.

The man smiled, the words he spoke in Cheyenne reminding Kelly of a verbal caress. The horse nipped at his shoulder, playfully this time. The man made a regretful sound when Bountiful shifted her attention to the palm of his hand and lipped it in search of a treat.

Kelly couldn't believe her eyes.

Joey stared, equally fascinated by the rapport between man and horse. "I guess he's not a criminal," he whispered.

The man jackknifed into a sitting position in one quick motion. His gaze wary as he studied his audience, he continued to stroke Bountiful's nose.

"Who are you, mister?" Joey asked, awe in his voice.

The man said nothing, simply stared at the boy.

Kelly took the opportunity to study the stranger. She registered the long black mane of hair that cascaded down his back, the width of his shoulders, the long-limbed lines of his muscular body, and the character etched into his strong, dark facial features.

He's not pretty, her senses shouted, but he's all man. Rugged. Raw-boned. Powerful, and not just in a physical sense.

Despite his current condition, Kelly suspected that he was capable of wrestling the elements for control and coming out the victor nine times out of ten. The expression on his face also assured her he was the kind of man capable of dominating others with the force of his personality and will. He looked vaguely primitive as well, almost as if he'd walked off the pages of a history book.

Get a grip, she told herself, amazed by the ludicrous thoughts filling her head. Squaring her slender shoulders, Kelly gave him a direct look, aware that the expression on her face was the one often described by her son as the *principal look*.

She doubted she could intimidate this man, but she intended to have an explanation for his presence.

"My name is Kelly Farrell. You're in my barn, which means you're on my land. I'd like to know why."

He got to his feet, all fluid grace and rippling muscles beneath the buckskin. Bountiful, female to the end, nuzzled his chest like a lover. He stroked her neck, his long, narrow fingers skimming over her, calming her, seducing her.

Kelly suddenly sensed then what his hands would feel like on a woman's body. She didn't even have to wonder. She just knew. She swallowed a startled gasp.

I've lost my mind, she decided in disgust.

"Mister, what happened to you?" Joey asked, unable to contain himself any longer as he slipped free of his mother's restraining hand and approached Bountiful's stall.

"Joseph!"

Joey glanced over his shoulder, clearly startled by his mother's sharp tone.

She gentled her voice with effort. "You need to finish packing for your trip."

"Aw, Mom."

"Now, please."

"But . . ."

"This isn't a debate, Joseph," she said, her tone soft, although it conveyed a wealth of parental authority.

"Yes, ma'am."

Joey kicked at a clump of hay in frustration before shrugging in the direction of the man in Bountiful's stall. Under his mother's watchful gaze, he turned and scuffed his way out of the barn.

The man observed the boy's departure. Kelly thought she saw a flash of sympathy in his eyes before he blinked and refocused on her.

"I've told you my name. I'd like you to identify yourself, and I'd like to know why you're in my barn."

His gaze penetrating, he said nothing as he guided Bountiful out of his way with a light touch, then brushed away the bits of hay clinging to his clothing. He exited the stall, his posture proud, although he moved with a telltale slowness that said his sturdy body felt the need to protest his use of his limbs.

Kelly didn't miss his grimace or the stiff manner in which he walked. "Are you all right?" she asked, concern warring with natural caution.

He paused once as he closed the metal gate, his fingers lingering briefly on the metal. He frowned before withdrawing his hand.

"Please answer me."

He jerked a nod in her direction.

"Who are you? Why are you here?"

He met her gaze, appraisal in his eyes as they boldly skimmed over her. Kelly sensed that he was taking more than her measure as a person.

His inspection annoyed her, but she kept her feelings to herself.

Frustrated by his silence, she persisted. "Are you hurt, aside from the burns on your arms?"

As though unaware of them until now, he glanced down at the angry red splotches on his forearms before he met her gaze again. "I am not injured." He shifted sideways, his movement very deliberate.

"Are you certain you aren't hurt? I've had first aid training, if you require basic medical care."

"I require nothing of you," he said, his tone formal, his accent hinting that he'd spent time on the East Coast.

"Who are you?" Kelly asked.

"No one of consequence to a white woman."

Kelly gaped at him. *A white woman?*

He hesitated, then drilled her with a penetrating look. "The boy. Joseph."

"What about him?"

"You are his mother?"

"Yes."

"You claim him openly?"

Confused, she said, "Of course—he's my son."

"He is a half-breed."

She felt as though she'd been slapped, and she stiffened. "That's an ugly label, and I won't tolerate it in my home."

"Label?" He repeated the word, his voice low, reflective.

The sound of rock music suddenly blasted into the quiet of the barn like exploding dynamite. Kelly flinched even though she recognized the sound. The music died as abruptly as it had begun, but the horses reacted with predictable uneasiness. Kelly held her breath until they settled down. Only then did she turn to glare at her red-faced son.

"Sorry, Mom. My finger slipped." Joey clutched his new CD player, a birthday gift from his grandparents the previous week.

"You should be sorry."

"Can I take it with me?"

"Yes. Please go back to the house."

"Uh, Mom."

"What is it now?" Kelly was too exasperated to pretend that she wasn't angry with his delaying tactics.

"Look."

She followed his gaze and immediately noticed the expression on the face of the strange man. Flattened against the wall, he looked stunned and ready to flee.

Without glancing at her son, she asked, "Joey, do you still want to go to camp?"

"I'm history, Mom." With that, he shot out of the barn at top speed.

Her attention still on their guest, Kelly sensed not just disorientation but genuine alarm. She didn't know why, but she felt compelled to make him feel more comfortable. "The music he likes gives me a headache too. Modern technology is a very mixed blessing."

"Not music."

She half-smiled. "I agree."

Some of the rigidity eased out his body, but his gaze remained cautious.

"I need to know why you're here."

"Sleep."

"That much I've figured out."

"I will leave now."

"I recognize you from last night."

He peered at her, although he didn't acknowledge her comment one way or another.

"You saved Martha Hurley's life. Were you visiting her?"

"Not by choice," he said.

What an odd answer, she thought. "What you did was quite heroic. Martha will want to thank you, as will her family."

"I am not a hero. I'm just a man . . . a man who doesn't . . ." His voice trailed off.

"Why didn't you stop when I called out to you?" She saw the uncertainty in his eyes as she finished speaking.

He suddenly slumped back against the wall, as though stricken with pain. Lifting his hands, he drove his fingers through his thick hair, the heels of his palms pressing against his temples. His eyes fell closed as he ground his jaws together.

The air in Kelly's lungs felt like a wedge of cement as she stared at him. She felt the pain that lanced through him even though she didn't understand the cause. Her concern about his welfare increased.

When he finally straightened and lifted his head, his dense mane of hair shifted across his shoulders and down his back, rippling like an unraveling bolt of obsidian silk.

Kelly stared in fascination, unable to draw her eyes from him. Rugged masculine grace showed in even the subtlest movement of his body. He was a midnight fantasy, the forbidden kind of fantasy capable of haunting a lonely woman. She paled, realizing that he resembled the unknown man who often invaded her dreams and made her too restless to sleep on hot summer nights.

The sound of frustration that emerged from him a few moments later brought her crashing back to the reality of the moment. "You obviously need to be checked over by a doctor," Kelly said.

His hands dropped like lead weights to his sides. He gave her a hard look. "I need nothing."

"Don't be so stubborn!" she hissed, some part of her still alert to the sensitive nature of the animals housed in the barn.

He stiffened, his expression growing stormy. It was clear to Kelly that he wasn't accustomed to being spoken to in that manner. She was beyond caring, though.

"Mom?"

Kelly swung around to face her son. "What are you trying to prove?"

The horses whinnied their collective distress.

Joey lowered his voice. "Nothing."

"Then what do you want?"

"He's a mess, Mom. He needs a shower, and he's prob'ly hungry."

"Joseph Michael Farrell . . ." she began.

"Maybe then he'll tell you his name," her son suggested with a sunny smile.

"We aren't running a hotel."

"Yes, ma'am."

"You're skating on thin ice, young man."

"You're always telling me it's better to be clean than dirty. Maybe he feels the same way."

She glanced at their guest, who seemed intrigued by their conversation. "My son has a point, even though it's a weak one. We can offer you a shower, clean clothing, and breakfast before you leave. In exchange for our hospitality, I would like to know your name and why you decided to spend the night in our barn." Kelly looked at Joey. "Check and see if there are clean towels in the hired man's quarters."

As he darted off, the man repeated a word she'd used. "Shower?"

She nodded, relieved that he was responding. "A shower first, and then your name. Do we have a deal?"

He nodded his agreement, although he didn't

budge from his position against the wall. He simply watched her as she walked toward him.

Kelly moved with the same care she used with skittish animals. Pausing in front of him, she quelled the frisson of sensory awareness that winnowed into her bloodstream. "Please extend your arms so I can check them for you."

Despite his initial hesitation, he did as she requested. Kelly examined both sides of his forearms, her experienced gaze assuring her that his burns weren't serious or in danger of blistering. She lingered over the scratches on his hands, then scanned the ones on his face.

"You'll be all right, but getting cleaned up should guarantee that these scratches don't become infected. I have some clothes my brother left the last time he visited us. The two of you are about the same size, so you can use his things after you shower if you'd like a fresh change of clothing."

He gripped her wrists when she started to step back. "Shower?"

His touch resonated through her like the aftermath of an explosion. Her gaze flew to his face, her heart tripping wildly beneath her breasts. She watched his eyes darken even as she registered the shock in them. She wondered then if her shock was as apparent. She suspected it was, but she was too shaken to think clearly for several moments.

Instead of trying to free herself, she calmly

said, "Yes, a shower. I suspect you'll feel better once you've had one."

The warmth of his skin continued to sink into her pores. She kept her gaze locked on his face as her pulse fluttered like an out-of-control kite and then went into a tailspin. No one had touched her in years. She hadn't wanted any man's touch since losing James, despite the periodic bouts of loneliness she experienced as a single mother.

She peered up at him, searching his face with eyes the color of deepest jade. She saw his confusion, felt it. "What's wrong?" she managed to ask, the compassion that flooded her heart infusing her voice with more gentleness than she realized.

He opened his mouth to speak, then snapped it shut. He shook his head, as though her question was too difficult to answer.

"If you tell me, perhaps I can . . ."

He interrupted her before she could say anything more. "Where is your man? And why are you clothed in such an unseemly manner?"

Kelly felt as though she'd been drenched in icewater. She stared at him, thinking how utterly sexist he sounded. Well, she reminded herself, he wasn't the first, and he certainly wouldn't be the last, to question her right to be part of a male-dominated world.

Joey chose that moment to reappear. "I found the towels, Mom."

Kelly pulled free of his hold at the sound of

her son's voice, although she couldn't find her own for a long moment. Turning, she summoned a smile for Joey, but her thoughts snagged on a question the stranger had asked. One word—a remarkably outdated word—blinked like a neon light in her head. *Unseemly?*

"Hey, mister, did my Mom tell you that my Dad was a real Cheyenne warrior? I never knew him, 'cause he died when I was a little kid, but I have pictures of him."

The man nodded, his expression sober, his eyes filled with torment.

Joey, with the artlessness of a child, approached him and took his hand. "I'll show you the way, okay? Did you know I'm going to sleep-away camp? I can't wait. It'll be my first time."

"Joseph . . . ," Kelly began, instinctively protective of her son.

He flashed an expectant look at her. "Yeah, Mom?"

The man paused, his gaze steady as he studied her. "I do not harm children." He spoke with quiet dignity.

He reads minds, too, she concluded. She realized, though, that she believed him. Her grandmother had once counseled her that she had to take some things on pure faith. Kelly decided this was one of those times. She gave her son a stern look. "Mind your manners. There's no need to talk his ear off."

"Aw, Mom."

"Breakfast in fifteen minutes. I'm going up to the house, but I'll be right back."

Joey grinned and tugged on the hand that engulfed his smaller one. "Come on, mister. Soon as you shower, we can have breakfast. My mom's a great cook."

Kelly almost told her son that she hardly needed references when providing a free meal. Instead, she made her way out of the barn, past the corral, and into the house. Every instinct she owned told her Joey was safe, even though this man was a stranger to them.

She smiled as she climbed the stairs to the guest room of the rambling old house she'd called home since the first weeks of her marriage. The real question was whether or not the man who'd spent the night with Bountiful was safe from Joey, the resident chatterbox. Kelly sincerely doubted it.

She returned to the barn less than five minutes later. The bathroom door was partially open, and she paused when she heard the running water and Joey's voice.

"My mom makes me shower every night before I go to bed. Can you believe it? She's terrific, but she's a total clean freak."

Kelly heard a muffled response as she knocked on the door and waited for Joey to answer it.

"I think it's a waste of water and soap, but she

doesn't agree. Clay, do you think all moms are like mine?"

Clay?

Because Joey ignored her second knock, Kelly peeked around the edge of the door, made sure their guest was still ensconced in the shower, then opened the door all the way. Clouds of soap-scented steam escaped the bathroom and briefly billowed around her before evaporating.

"Joey?"

He turned and flashed a bright smile in her direction. "Yeah, Mom?"

"Clean clothes. Everything all right in here?"

"Yeah, Clay's prob'ly almost done."

"Good."

She slid the folded jeans and shirt onto the countertop of a cupboard just inside the door, but she froze when the water stopped. Before she could duck out of the bathroom, her guest pushed open the shower door.

She stared at him. She couldn't help herself. She couldn't move, either, despite the commands she issued to her feet.

Naked, beautifully formed, and soaking wet, he peered back at her. He didn't bother to conceal his body. Nor did he reach for the towel hanging over the shower door. He simply waited and watched her.

Feeling rooted to the floor, she averted her eyes.

"Mom, I couldn't find my flashlight. Have you seen it?"

"It's in the kitchen," she managed. "Breakfast is in five minutes. Don't take any side trips on your way to the house."

She hurriedly backed out of the bathroom and jerked the door closed. The image of his sculpted male anatomy stayed with her as she made her way to the house. It lingered as she set the table, warmed the scrambled eggs, made toast, poured orange juice, and perked a fresh pot of coffee.

Embarrassed when her son and Clay walked into the kitchen, she almost left the room, good manners be damned. In the end, she behaved as though nothing inappropriate had occurred.

THREE

Clay watched the boy's mother place a platter of eggs and bacon on the table beside a bowl of melon slices. Relieved that he recognized the food being served, he perused the rest of the room.

While the indoor water pump and cupboards made sense to him, he didn't recognize many of the other furnishings in the kitchen. Clay didn't intend to reveal his ignorance. Ignorance, he'd learned, often gave the less scrupulous an advantage.

Joey slipped into a chair at the table. "Come on, Clay. Your food'll get cold."

The stranger hesitated, his gaze shifting to his hostess.

After retrieving a coffee pot and filling two mugs, Kelly glanced at him. "Please sit down, Mr. . . ."

Under other circumstances, he might have smiled at her determination to have him reveal his identity. He respected strength, and she clearly possessed that particular character trait. He decided that the name given him by his stepfather would suffice. "Sloan. Clayton Sloan, Mrs. Farrell."

"Mr. Sloan," she repeated.

"Yes."

"Please call me Kelly," she invited. "We're very informal at the breakfast table."

The etiquette he'd learned in Boston had become second nature to him over the years, so he approached the table and pulled out her chair before she could reach for it. Her startled smile amused him, but the sound of her voice when she said "Thank you" stirred a longing in his heart that surprised and momentarily disconcerted him.

It was not his habit to desire a white woman, but he felt desire for Kelly Farrell. He knew now he'd been mistaken. She was not a demon. She was a striking, auburn-haired woman of at least thirty winters with a half-breed child—a child she obviously loved.

She was also a woman who owned property, apparently due to the death of her husband, and a woman who clothed herself in man's attire and revealed her feminine form. The latter habit unsettled him and made him aware of the unruly impulses surging hotly through his bloodstream each time he looked at her.

The scent of her skin reminded him of the hothouse orchids his mother had grown during his years in Boston. The fragrance, like Kelly, had a seductive impact on his senses, despite his effort to ignore both.

Kelly Farrell was a woman of courage, he realized as he took his place at the table and reached for the napkin beside his plate. She had trusted him with her son, and she had welcomed him into her home to dine at her table.

Clay didn't understand the reasons for her trust or her hospitality. He knew he probably never would. Once he'd eaten, he planned to depart.

This spirit world made no sense to him—if, in fact, it was a true spirit world. He'd begun to doubt it for two very simple reasons: he experienced physical pain, and he felt hunger. His instincts assured him those two things were not part of the afterlife.

Although he had no idea where he was, Clay sensed that he'd somehow been transported to a place and time beyond his comprehension. He felt compelled to seek an understanding of what had happened to him, but in private, and only after a ritual cleansing in the tradition of the Cheyenne.

"Are you packed?" Kelly asked, her gaze on her son.

"Yeah, except for my flashlight."

"It's on the counter behind you," she told him as she served herself from the platter in the center of the table.

"Maybe Clay would like to be our new hired man, Mom."

As he sank his teeth into a chunk of melon, Clay glanced at the woman, who seemed as disconcerted as he was by her son's remark.

"I'm sure Mr. Sloan already has a job, Joey."

"Do you, Clay?" the boy asked. "I bet you train horses like my Mom, don't you?"

He hesitated, his thoughts on the law practice he'd left behind in Boston. "I was employed until recently," he answered, without revealing the nature of his profession or expounding on the fact that the Cheyenne had once been known for their skill with horses.

"Are you on vacation?" Joey persisted between mouthfuls of food.

Clay responded to the boy, aware he was expressing the curiosity typical of any child. "I was returning to my people."

"Do you have relatives near here?" Kelly asked.

"I did," he said, nearly choking on the anguish that surged up inside him. Fighting for control over his emotions, Clay fell silent and struggled with his memories of the devastation he'd discovered at Sand Creek.

"Couldn't you locate them?" Kelly asked,

reaching for a slice of toast and then passing the dish to him.

He accepted the plate and took a piece of toast. "They . . . they are not a part of this world." Clay dropped his gaze to the food in front of him. As he reached for his fork, a tremor shook his hand. He closed it into a fist, determined to master his emotions.

"Are you all right?" Kelly asked, her voice soft, her eyes revealing genuine concern.

Clay exhaled. "Yes, thank you."

"You must have been very disappointed to discover they'd moved away. Perhaps Joey and I knew them."

"It is doubtful," he said before sampling the eggs.

"When's Aunt Jenny supposed to get here, Mom?" Joey asked.

"Soon, so finish your breakfast."

"Yes, ma'am." He shoveled another forkful of eggs into his mouth.

"Mr. Sloan, your native clothing appears to be authentic. I don't think I've ever seen buckskins so well preserved. Did you inherit them from your family?"

"The clothing is mine," he said tersely, not bothering to tell her that the material was elkskin.

"I didn't mean to imply that it wasn't," Kelly calmly remarked after taking a sip of coffee.

Clay told himself to relax. She wasn't accusing him of theft. She was making conversation. "They were made for me."

"The stitching and beadwork are exquisite."

"Thank you."

"Did you know my dad, Clay?"

"It is unlikely," he answered, his expression revealing his compassion for the fatherless boy.

"My mom says he was a neat guy."

Clay looked at Kelly as he pondered the word *neat*. He connected it to cleanliness and order, but the boy obviously had another meaning in mind.

"Your father was a wonderful man, Joey," she said gently. "He loved you very much, and he would have been proud of you."

Joey sat a little taller in his chair and grinned at his mother before looking at Clay. "I kinda look like him, too."

"It is good that you take pride in your heritage," Clay said, surprised by the respect he saw in the faces of the boy and his mother.

"I'm half Cheyenne. Mom says that's my best half, but I'm not supposed to say that in front of Grandpa and Grandma Jennings."

Clay peered at Kelly. "Your family disapproved of your marriage?"

She nodded, her regret apparent. "At first."

"This saddened you," he observed, startled by the possibility.

"Very much," she admitted. "James was patient with them, though. He reminded me that people fear what they don't understand. He was a strong man, strong enough to look past the prejudice that exists in our world."

"You cared for him." It wasn't a question, but a statement of fact with an undertone of shock.

Kelly smiled. "I loved him."

"Me too," added Joey.

Clay studied the boy. "Your mother is right. Your father would have been proud of you. It is right that you honor his memory."

"Anybody home?" sang out a feminine voice.

Clay stiffened with alarm.

The woman attached to the voice burst into the kitchen like a whirlwind, long braids flying behind her, skirts swirling like a rainbow around her legs. "All set for camp, Joey, my love?"

"You bet, Aunt Jenny." After gulping down the last of his juice, he shot to his feet and grabbed his flashlight from the counter behind his chair.

"Hi, there." The new arrival openly inspected the man seated at Kelly's breakfast table.

Clay got to his feet, surprised anew because of the woman's tribal heritage and her entry into the Farrell home without a formal invitation. "Good morning."

"This is Clayton Sloan, Jenny." Kelly smiled. "Clay, Jenny is my sister-in-law."

The woman remarked, "It's good to see a man in this kitchen."

Kelly flushed. "Be nice."

Joey tugged on Jenny's arm. "Don't you think Clay would make a great hired man for Mom?"

Jenny's smile widened. "The idea definitely gets my vote." She patted the boy's shoulder. "Get your stuff, kiddo. We're late, and your cousins are starting to remind me of wild Indians."

Clay frowned at the slur. He said nothing, however.

Kelly got up from the table and crossed the room to embrace her sister-in-law. "Thanks for taking him with you."

"No problem. You're exhausted from playing firefighter extraordinaire in the middle of the night. Besides, he's a coma case compared to my three." To Joey, she said, "Where's your suitcase?"

"In the front room."

Kelly turned to Clay. "Why don't you finish your breakfast while I say good-bye to Joey?"

"Nice to meet you, Clayton Sloan," Jenny tossed over her shoulder as she left the kitchen. "I hope you'll hang around. Kelly needs a good man . . ."

"Jennifer Farrell Lonetree!"

". . . to help with the horses," she finished.

Clay nodded warily, still standing as they all trooped out. Sitting once again, he listened to the conversation taking place in the living room.

"Make Clay stay, Mom. He's really nice, and he's good with horses."

"Out of the mouths of babes," Jenny chimed in.

"I can't order the man to work for me," Kelly insisted.

"Mom, I could ask him for you. Want me to?"

"I appreciate your offer, but I think you should concentrate on camp."

"I'll interview him for you," Jenny volunteered.

"You two are about as subtle as an avalanche," Kelly complained.

"So sue us," Jenny invited. "James would be furious if he knew you'd been alone all these years."

"Jenny!"

"Don't you *Jenny* me, Kelly Farrell. We both know I'm right."

Clay noticed that Kelly wasn't inclined to continue the discussion when she shifted her attention to her son. He couldn't help wondering why she hadn't taken another man.

"Time to go, sweetie. You have a great time."

"Aw, Mom, maybe I should stay home with you and Clay. I don't want to miss any good stuff."

"Does that mean you're going to miss me?" Kelly teased.

Clay smiled at her question as he massaged the pulse that had begun to batter his temple. He recalled how often his mother had teased him in a similar manner during his childhood.

"Prob'ly."

Jenny's laughter echoed through the lower level of the house. "Head 'em up and move 'em out, Master Joey. Sleep-away camp is our next stop."

Their voices faded. Clay heard a door slam.

Reaching for his coffee mug, he drained the contents. His body ached, as did his head. He still needed nourishment, but he felt too sick to his stomach to bother with it at the moment. He gritted his teeth, then shoved himself to his feet, intent on walking off the escalating physical discomfort invading his limbs.

The pain he'd experienced the previous night streaked like bolts of lightning through his body yet again, sapping him of energy and kicking his respiration into overdrive. The need for sleep dominated his consciousness, even though he knew he should be on his way. Weaving like a drunk, Clay started across the kitchen.

It took all his concentration to put one foot in front of the other. He moved with exaggerated care. Dizziness made the room tilt and blur. He blinked against the double vision that followed. Certain he was about to fall to his knees, he grabbed the wall for support.

When he was able to focus again, the calendar tacked to the wall beside the screen door was the first thing he noticed. At first what he read made no sense to him at all, but then it started to seem remotely possible. He didn't want to believe his eyes, and he resisted, but some instinct told him he must believe—must accept this reality.

He groaned, shock and disbelief resonating in the sound. *It can't be*, Clay told himself. The year on the calendar could not be correct.

Kelly waved to Joey and his boisterous cousins as her sister-in-law headed off in her late-model minivan. The vehicle left a trail of dust in its wake as Jenny navigated the rutted dirt road leading out to the highway.

Although she missed Joey already, Kelly felt confident he would enjoy his time at sleep-away camp. She comforted herself with a reminder that she and Jenny were scheduled to visit the children on Parents' Day, halfway through their stay.

She sensed that James would have approved of the camp they'd chosen for the kids. Designed to highlight the Cheyenne culture, the camp would allow her son and his cousins to expand their knowledge of their heritage while having fun in a supervised environment.

Kelly walked into the kitchen a few moments later, her thoughts on finishing her breakfast and on the chores she needed to do before taking the nap she'd been promising herself since returning from the Hurley fire shortly after dawn. She paused when she spotted Clay. Head bowed, he kneaded his temples with his fingertips as his large body visibly trembled.

Having witnessed him in this condition earlier in the barn, she suspected his headache had returned with a vengeance. She periodically suffered from severe tension headaches and knew they could disable even the sturdiest person.

"Clay? Are you all right? I can take you to the hospital if you'd like."

He didn't respond.

"Clay?" Kelly said once more.

He failed to respond, so she approached him. Standing behind him, she placed her hand on his shoulder to gain his attention. She decided to urge him to return to the hired man's quarters in the barn for more rest, but his reaction to her touch wiped that thought, and nearly everything else, from her mind.

He turned and grabbed her by the shoulders. The force with which he shoved her against the wall, combined with the panic in his eyes and his fierce grip, produced a startled gasp from Kelly.

"What is this place?" he demanded.

Stunned, she stared up at him.

"Answer me!"

"My ranch," she managed.

"No!" he shouted, shaking her until her head bobbed. "Where am I?"

Anger displaced her shock. Adrenaline and instinct guiding her, Kelly brought her arms up and slammed her fists into his midsection. "How dare you . . ."

He reacted as though she'd lightly tapped him. He controlled her easily, shackling her wrists with his strong hands and jerking her to a spot between his powerful thighs. "Where?"

Furious, Kelly refused to acquiesce. "Take your hands off me this instant."

A crack in the veneer of his anger appeared.

Kelly saw his confusion, saw as well how real his disorientation seemed.

"Please tell me," he choked out, sounding desperate.

Because he was just barely in control of himself, she supplied the answer. "We're about ten miles from the town of Holly Grove, Colorado."

"You are not a demon."

She laughed. She couldn't help herself, but the sound of her humor faded just a few seconds later, because she realized he was quite serious. "My students have called me worse, I suspect."

He frowned. "You are a teacher?"

"I was, but now I'm the principal of Joey's school."

"What else?"

She ticked off the short list that popped into her head. She didn't know what else to do. "A widow, part-time horse trainer, and full-time mother of a ten-year-old boy." She ran out of things she was willing to say, especially since *lonely thirty-four-year-old female who secretly longs for another chance at loving and being loved* wasn't an admission she felt inclined to verbalize. It was enough that she'd come to terms with that happy little fact herself in recent years.

"You are many things, but who are you?" he pressed.

"You already know my name," she reminded him, not really answering him. Sometimes, even she wondered who she was, especially late at night when sleep remained elusive and her thoughts wandered to what it might be like to share her life with the right man.

"Kelly Jennings Farrell."

"That's right. And I have the Irish temper the name implies when I'm pushed too hard," she cautioned. "What else do you want to know?"

Something was terribly wrong with Clayton Sloan, but instead of distancing herself from him and instead of feeling fear, she felt the need to help him. She prayed she wasn't behaving fool-ishly.

"Kelly," he said again, his hold on her wrists easing.

She tugged her hands free, but she remained standing in front of him. "Yes, Clay. Can you tell me what happened while I was saying good-bye to Joey? I was only gone for three or four min-utes."

His gaze narrowed. He studied her in the mo-ments that followed with an intensity that nor-mally would have made her uncomfortable.

Oddly, Kelly didn't mind his intent perusal. She welcomed it, because he seemed to be calming himself. As she looked up at him, she wondered what he saw in her expression.

Fear? Worry? Compassion? Perhaps some blending of all three emotions? She hoped he hadn't noticed the other telltale emotions moving through her—the steadily escalating attraction that kept taking her by surprise every time she even glanced at him, the desire that heated her flesh and made her aware of feminine needs long ignored.

The ticking of the stove clock finally broke the spell that had settled over her. Flushing, thanks to the direction of her thoughts, she drew in a steadying breath. "No one wants to harm you, Clay. You don't need to be afraid. . . ."

He interrupted her, his tone brusque. "Fear is not what I feel."

"Then what exactly are you feeling?" She spoke softly, then awaited his reply.

"Confusion," he finally answered. "Great confusion."

"Why?"

"The reasons are many," he admitted.

"Can you be a little more specific?"

"What is the year?"

Surprised by his question, she repeated it: " 'What is the year?' "

"Yes."

Kelly told him.

"That is not possible."

"Look at the calendar, if you don't believe me," she urged.

Anger defined the angles of his face more clearly. "It lies. *You* lie, Kelly Farrell."

"I have no reason to lie to you."

He pressed his fingertips to his temples again, then closed his eyes.

Peering up at him, Kelly marveled not for the first time at the denseness of his eyelashes, the rugged contours of his features, and the silky-looking black mane that spilled down his back. "Is Clay your real name, or did you make it up?" she asked.

He lowered his hands. "Clayton Sloan is the name given to me as a boy by my stepfather. It is the name I use in the white world."

White world? Why does he keep making that distinction? she wondered. "What is your real name?"

"Why?"

"Because I want to know."

"I am not a curiosity to be displayed for your amusement. I am a man."

Tell me something I don't already know, she thought, her pulse picking up speed while a feeling that reminded her of hot syrup spilling into her bloodstream threatened to submerge her senses. "I know that, Clay."

He straightened, squaring his shoulders. He spoke with quiet dignity. "I am Cloud Dancer."

"Thank you for trusting me."

"I am repaying your trust with your son."

"You're Cheyenne, aren't you?"

He nodded warily, as though she might use that revelation against him.

"Is that why you came here? To reacquaint yourself with your roots?"

"I did not come here by choice."

"Now I'm really confused. Are you telling me you were brought to Colorado against your will?"

"I did not seek this place or this time."

As she wrestled with yet another of his question-producing replies, Kelly continued to search for a rational explanation for his situation. "You said earlier you were visiting your family."

He drew in a ragged breath. The tortured quality of the sound made her heart ache.

"They are with the Great Spirit."

"Are you telling me they've all died?"

Torment unlike anything she'd ever seen filled his eyes. "They were massacred. All of them."

Massacred? "You found them," she said softly.

"Yes."

"When?"

"Yesterday, I think."

Yesterday? Have I fallen into the Twilight Zone? she wondered. Proceeding cautiously, she asked, "Are we talking about a lot of people?"

"Hundreds," he ground out. "So many that I stopped counting the bodies."

Chilled by his statement, Kelly knew what she had to do. "I'd better call the sheriff for you. He needs to speak to you about the fire at Martha's house, anyway."

"I will not be hanged for an act of charity," he said angrily.

"Hanged?" she burst out, certain now she was on the verge of slipping into some kind of insane time warp. She pressed on, despite her confusion, because he seemed to believe what he was saying to her. "You aren't making any sense, Clay. You saved Martha Hurley's life. People will want to thank you. And if you found . . ."

"No," he shouted as he turned away from her and reached for the screen door handle. "My people have been hanged for far less. It is not a fate I envision for myself."

Kelly grabbed his arm.

He staggered, then grasped his head with both hands. "The pain will not stop."

A worrisome thought occurred to her. She'd dealt with mental health issues as a teacher and as a grade school principal. "Have you been hospitalized recently?"

"I am in excellent health. I have no need of hospitals or the charlatans who run them. Their medicine is bad."

"That isn't quite what I meant," Kelly began, no longer put off by his archaic choice of words as she tried to get the information she needed without sending him over some psychological cliff.

Closing his eyes, he fell back against the wall, then slowly sank to his knees. He moaned.

Kelly dropped down to kneel in front of him. Without thinking, she reached out and framed his hard-featured face with her hands. "Clay, what can I do to help you?"

He looked at her, his dark eyes skimming over her face.

Kelly sensed he could see into her soul. Instead of speaking, she simply waited for him to grasp a simple truth: that she posed no threat to him.

They studied each other in silence for several moments.

As she waited for him to answer her question, she absorbed the warmth of his skin as it sank into her palms and fingers. She wanted to reassure him everything would be all right, but she knew better than to weave fantasies in the face of reality. And reality for now was a deeply troubled man who evoked feelings she hadn't experienced in a very long time.

"You cannot help me. No one can," he said finally.

She understood what he meant. Some things couldn't be helped or fixed, but she intended to try. "Will you trust me?"

"Why?"

Kelly smiled gently. "Because you can."

"Why?" he asked again.

"I understand pain, especially the emotional kind. When Joey's father died, I felt overwhelmed and without hope. It took me a long time to recover from those feelings, but I eventually did."

"You do not understand," he insisted, his temper flaring.

"Is it necessary to understand in order to feel compassion?"

Stiffening, he knocked her hands away from his face. "Do not pity me."

"I don't," she insisted. "You are not the kind of man a woman pities."

"What are you proposing?" he asked, his fingers straying to his temples.

"You obviously need to rest and regain your strength. You can use the hired man's quarters in the barn. It's a small studio apartment. It's not fancy, but it's clean. After you get some sleep, we can discuss your options."

He frowned. "Options?"

"Choices," she clarified. "For now, though, why don't you concentrate on resting? Your thoughts will be much clearer then."

"Why are you willing to assist me?"

"Is there some reason I shouldn't?" she asked. "Do you intend to harm me?"

He pushed to his feet, his pride evident in his

posture. "It is not my way to harm women or children."

"I believe you," Kelly said as she stood and faced him.

His gaze narrowed. "You will not summon the sheriff?"

She shook her head. "You have my word of honor."

His tone of voice was scathing as he spoke. "There is little honor in the world."

"Don't be so cynical."

"You speak strangely," he remarked.

"Fine minds think alike," she quipped, her thoughts not just on his formal-sounding speech patterns but on the way he used certain outdated words. It was as though he were from the last century, at the very least from another decade, but that wasn't possible. Was it?

You're exhausted and your imagination has gone haywire, a voice in her head announced. She suspected the voice had a point. Two points, she amended.

Following a last searching look, Clay turned away from her, his broad shoulders filling the doorway as he pushed open the screen door. He paused, then looked back at her.

"What?" she asked softly, unable to stop herself from delaying his departure.

"I came here last night because I didn't know where else to go. My world is lost to me."

The stark expression on his face assured Kelly

that he believed he spoke the truth. She believed him, in fact, although more from instinct than reason.

As she watched him walk to the barn, she recalled his disbelief when she'd told him the year. Kelly wondered what year he thought it should be. She made a mental note to find out, then walked back into the kitchen, gathered up the breakfast dishes, and piled them in the sink.

Her unexpected guest remained in her thoughts as she climbed the stairs to the master suite and stretched out atop her bed. Later, she decided as she drifted off to sleep, later she would solve the puzzle posed by one Clayton Sloan, the man also known as Cloud Dancer.

FOUR

A nightmare held him in thrall. He fought for his freedom, searching frantically for an escape route out of the consuming darkness.

Clay awoke suddenly, gasping for air. Sweat streaked his face and chest. He sensed a presence nearby. Without thinking, he seized the entity as it hovered over him, jerked it downward, and used his body to restrain it.

He heard a muffled yelp.

The spirit resisted his efforts to subdue it, but his superior strength assured him he would emerge the victor in this contest.

"Clay!"

The sound of his name startled him. So did the voice when he recognized it.

"You're crushing me!"

He immediately realized what he'd done. Rolling off Kelly, he kept her anchored to the bed with one hand and the weight of a muscular, jeans-clad thigh. "Explain yourself," he ordered.

"Let go of me," she insisted, ignoring his command with a stubbornness that might have amused him under other circumstances.

Still wary of her motives, he asked, "Why?"

She made a sound rich with exasperation. "So I can turn on the light."

Aware that she posed no physical threat, he freed one of her hands. He blinked against the sudden glare of the light, his narrowed gaze snagging on the source of illumination on the small table beside the bed. Although he'd noticed it earlier, he hadn't discerned it as a light source. He catalogued the information for later investigation and use. He already knew he had much to learn about this new world.

"You've got to stop tackling me every five seconds."

He peered down at her. Her auburn hair reminded him of a halo of muted flame. A flush tinted her fair skin, and fury made her green eyes sparkle.

He felt a quickening deep in his belly. His loins swelled, the blood flowing through his body rapidly heating. He shifted his hips, unwilling to reveal to her the power she wielded over his flesh and his senses.

"Are you going to let me up?" Kelly asked tersely.

Clay nodded, released her, and sat up.

She scrambled off the bed, jerking her sweater into place as she glared at him.

He inclined his head. "Why are you here?"

"To check on you, of course. You've been asleep for almost twelve hours. You missed supper, so I fixed you a tray."

"Thank you," he said as he massaged his temples.

"Does your head still ache?"

He lowered his hands. The sudden softening of her voice tantalized him, but he quelled his reaction to her. "Less now."

"I'm relieved to hear that. I've been worried about you."

He liked her concern, he realized as he watched her walk across the room.

"You must be hungry."

Struck anew by the willowy grace of her body, he nodded absently. Her slender limbs and hourglass shape, visible thanks to the clothing she wore, roused a visceral response that made him want to abandon all caution and take her.

She tempted him greatly. He sensed he could lose himself within her. He doubted the wisdom of such behavior, though, especially with this woman. She had the nature of a hellion.

Irritated with himself, Clay demanded, "Why do you dress in this manner?"

"I dress for practicality," she said, sounding matter-of-fact as she glanced at him.

"It is practical," he conceded, "but is it proper?"

She chuckled as she removed the cover from one of the dishes on the tray. "The only time propriety becomes an issue is if I decide to stroll down Main Street in my birthday suit. That kind of behavior is frowned on when you're a grade school principal. The school board would send me packing in short order."

"Birthday suit?"

"Stark naked," she amended, frowning slightly as she scanned his features. "I'm not inclined to do that, so we don't have a problem. Besides, women have all the rights men possess."

The thought of her naked and his flesh buried in her softness aroused him yet again. Angry now with himself, he cursed his willful thoughts. "All?" he asked, shifting his attention to her final comment.

"All," she confirmed. "We're equal under the law."

"Much about the law has changed, then," he observed, thinking of the profession he'd pursued before leaving Boston.

"A very long time ago." She grinned. "Men are still trying to adjust."

Clay had no doubt about that. "This amuses you?"

"Not really. It's how the gender wars probably started. My women friends are of the opinion that they'll never end."

"There is a war?"

"In a manner of speaking, but you don't need to worry about it." Her gaze shifted away from his bare chest.

It was not the first time she'd had difficulty with the fact that he was attired in nothing more than the trousers she'd supplied, Clay realized.

Kelly cleared her throat.

"There is a problem?" he asked, even though he knew the exact nature of her discomfort. He felt vaguely pleased to know he wasn't the only one unsettled by awareness.

"Perhaps you should put on your shirt."

For that brief moment, Clay realized they were simply a man and a woman. The realization was oddly reassuring. "Of course." He reached for the shirt she'd loaned him earlier. Slipping into it, he didn't bother to fasten the buttons.

"I'll be in the barn. You're welcome to join me when you've finished eating."

"Stay." He spoke more sharply than he intended, primarily because it embarrassed him to want her company.

She paused in the open doorway. "Why?"

"Why not?" he asked, mimicking her question of earlier in the day to cover the awkwardness he felt.

"Interesting question," she murmured as she took a seat at the table for two.

Joining her at the table, Clay sampled the

food—a seasoned beef stew, warm biscuits, and a glass of milk. "You are an excellent cook."

"One of my many talents," Kelly said with a smile.

"And the others?"

Her smile faded. "I'll give you a list."

He concentrated on the meal, although he remained alert to his surroundings and her silence. "You are angry again?"

"No."

"What, then?"

She chewed on the inside of her cheek. "Concerned is a better word."

He paused, placing his fork on the plate and setting aside his napkin. "You feel unsafe in my presence?"

Kelly shook her head. "Of course not."

He waited, sensing by the expression on her face that she was carefully weighing her words.

"Why were you so upset by the date on the calendar?" she finally asked.

He shoved the plate aside as he surged to his feet. Stalking across the room, he paused at the window and peered out into the darkness.

"Clay?"

He flinched at the sound of her voice, surprised that she'd come up behind him without his being aware of her approach.

She touched his arm. "I'm not trying to upset you."

He turned slowly. Her hand slid away, although she didn't step back. He longed to call back her touch, but he cautioned himself against such foolishness.

They were from different worlds.

Perhaps even different centuries.

"You do, though," he muttered, his gaze locked on her upturned face, his hands beyond his control as he skimmed his fingertips up her arms. "You upset me in ways no other woman ever has." Especially a white woman, he finished silently.

He curved his hands over her shoulders.

She trembled.

He felt it.

Her eyes fell closed.

He waited.

A sigh washed past her slightly parted lips.

He instinctively leaned down, hungry to experience the flavor of the delicate sound.

"What are you . . ." Her voice trailed off.

He framed her face with hands that shook.

She stared up at him, her eyes huge with shock but also a hint of some emotion that appeared to be recognition. Her breathing became so shallow that he thought she might suffer a case of the vapors.

"Clay?" she whispered.

He knew he was behaving with uncharacteristic recklessness as he leaned closer, but he couldn't control the impulses seething within his body. He claimed the promise of her lips in the next heartbeat.

She tasted of sweetness and comfort and salvation. She tasted of other things as well, things that shocked him—welcome and desire. He drank in her hunger for what he offered, her response to him igniting his senses and hardening his body so quickly that he felt momentarily off balance.

She inched closer, aligning her body to his more powerful one. Her pelvis pressed against his loins. Pleasure lanced through him, then rocked him right down to the soles of his feet. He circled her shoulders with his arms, groaning when he felt her breasts plump against his chest.

His heart raced. His body burned.

She gripped his narrow waist, her lips parting even more as she angled her head. "Yes. Oh, yes," she breathed against his mouth.

Had he imagined her words? he wondered. Or had he simply heard the echo of his own desire?

As if sensing his hesitation, Kelly deepened their kiss.

Clay accepted her invitation and sank into her heat, his tongue slipping into her mouth to chart the damp interior. His hunger for her escalated with every passing second, and he quickly discovered he couldn't get enough of her.

She moaned into his mouth.

He inhaled that sound and all the other delicate noises she made, all the while basking in her responsiveness. He savored the honesty of her passion. He realized Kelly Farrell was no coy little miss out to tease a man and then accuse him of trying to take advantage of her. This was a woman who knew what she wanted.

He felt her hands slide up his back beneath his shirt, her fingertips kneading his muscular flesh. She explored him, and her touch made his blood flow like rivers of steam heat.

He longed to strip away the clothing that separated them, just as he longed to know every orchid-scented inch of her skin. He held back, though, despite the torment caused by his restraint. He was not the kind of man who rushed a woman once he claimed her. He preferred to linger, to savor.

He clasped her hips with his hands, bringing her into more intimate contact with his swollen loins. Holding her still, he shifted against her, back and forth, back and forth, until the contact sent charges of near-disabling sensation into every cell of his body.

As he acquainted her with the depth of his desire, she clutched at his back. Her body trembled. He wanted to absorb her into his pores, so great was his need as she undulated against him.

A few moments later, without warning, she wrenched her mouth free.

Clay felt an acute sense of loss.

Kelly gasped for breath, although she made

no effort to separate their shaking bodies. If anything, she clung to him more fiercely than before.

He held her then, resting his forehead against hers while they both fought for control. Too stunned by the force of his desire for her and the volatility of her response to do anything else, Clay remained silent. The intimacy they'd just shared had felt so right.

Kelly finally lifted her head and peered up at Clay.

He met her gaze but didn't speak. For a man known as a skilled orator, he felt unable to form a single coherent sentence as he searched her features for some hint of her state of mind.

"Let me help you make some sense of what's happened to you," she urged softly.

Clay felt as though he'd walked into a slamming door. He abandoned her where she stood, his emotions in disarray and his self-protective instincts gathering around him like a band of warriors willing to fight to the death to guarantee his survival.

Kelly followed him across the room. "Wait, please."

He shook loose of her when she grabbed his arm.

She persisted. "Clay! I just want to help you."

He whirled on her, anger etched into the angular lines of his face and evident in the tension invading his powerful body, a body still aroused to the point of pain. "I don't want help, especially from a woman."

She stumbled to a stop. "This is the twentieth century, Clayton Sloan, and I suggest you not forget it."

"This is some future version of hell," he countered, his temper emerging. "And don't tell me again that men and women are equal," he warned. "The concept is wasted on me."

"You'd better revise your thinking, then."

"Men and women are too different ever to be equal."

Kelly took a steadying breath, then spoke candidly, "I celebrate the obvious physical differences, Clay." She closed the distance between them. "What just happened between us proves that there are differences."

"Why did you let me kiss you?" he demanded, feeling like a fool the instant the words left his mouth.

"For the same reason you kissed me," she answered.

He scowled at her.

"It's what we both wanted."

Her honesty surprised him yet again, but then he wondered if her replies to any of his questions were motivated by things he didn't yet understand. Feeling disadvantaged angered and unsettled him, and he didn't try to conceal his emotions.

"Where are you from?" she asked.

He both resented and admired her persistence. It spoke to the strength of her character. "That does not concern you."

"Boston, perhaps?" she pressed.

He gave her a wary look. "I lived there for many years," he grudgingly admitted, "but I am not *from* there."

"Where?"

He shook his head, but he wondered for a moment if he dared tell this woman the truth. He was from the past, and he had no future. He decided against saying anything more. "How did you know I had lived in Boston?"

"Your accent."

"I have none."

She smiled. "You definitely sound like an Easterner to me."

"I am Cheyenne. That is all you need to know."

"I need to know a heck of a lot more than that if you intend to stay here, and my instincts assure me you need to sit tight and figure out what's happened to you."

Sit tight? "Your words are designed to confuse."

"What are you talking about?" she exclaimed. "I'm just offering to help you."

Clay rubbed his temples, then made his way to the nearest chair, which he sank into like a man too exhausted to stay on his feet. He leaned forward, resting his elbows on his knees as he stared at the floor. "I thought I was dead. I believed I was entering the afterlife. Instead . . ."

"Instead?" Kelly encouraged as she dropped to her knees in front of him.

"Instead, I am in your world now. A world that makes little sense to me."

"Have you been out of the country?"

"Abroad?" he clarified.

Frowning, Kelly nodded.

"I toured the continent when I finished reading law at Harvard."

"Say that again," she requested.

He complied. Her stunned expression prompted him to ask, "Is something amiss?"

"What was the year, Clay?"

He hesitated.

She slid her hands into his, palm to palm.

He gripped them tightly, then gentled his touch when he saw her wince.

"Trust me, please," she urged once again.

He spoke then of his departure from Boston, the number of days and nights spent aboard trains and a series of stagecoaches, and his arrival in Denver, although he still hesitated to reveal the year of his journey. Nor did he mention what he'd discovered at Sand Creek. He couldn't speak of the devastation. Not yet, anyway. The pain he felt was still too intense.

"The year, Clay. Tell me the year."

"Why is the year so important to you?"

"Because it's obviously very important to you."

He capitulated, not altogether certain why as he told her what she wanted to know.

Her shock evident, Kelly stared at him for a full minute before whispering, "Merciful heaven. You're serious, aren't you?"

"I do not lie."

"Of course, you don't lie. It's just that . . . I don't . . ." She gave him a helpless look and lapsed into silence as she studied him.

"I am from the past, Kelly Farrell, and I am not a spirit. I am a flesh-and-blood man. I am real." Clay knew he was stating the obvious, but he felt compelled to confirm the truth as he understood it. He owed this woman that much, and probably much more.

Saying the words aloud also helped him accept the situation in which he now found himself. He silently prayed that the Great Spirit, in whose hands he felt certain his fate rested, would guide him, just as it had guided him since his delivery into this future world.

Still looking stunned, Kelly searched his face, then nodded.

As he watched her, Clay sensed she'd reached a conclusion.

"As crazy as I probably sound, I believe you, even though I can't explain why or how. Where you're concerned, I'm operating on pure instinct."

Relieved and reassured by her words, Clay voiced the worry that had haunted him since that morning. "The sheriff."

"What about him?" Kelly asked.

"You will speak to him now?"

"Is that what you want me to do?"

Clay shook his head. "No."

"Then I won't."

"I still have no wish to be hanged."

"That won't happen," she insisted. "You're talking about frontier justice, and that's part of our history."

He pushed to his feet and stepped past her. "I have witnessed that kind of justice. I saw it as a boy, and I have seen it as a man."

Kelly stood and followed him.

"Speak," he said, aware thanks to the pensive expression on her face that she had more to say.

She paused just a few steps from him. "I haven't betrayed you, and I don't plan to start now."

He measured her sincerity with the benefit of years of courtroom experience at his disposal, years spent deftly questioning witnesses who thought they were far more learned about the law than he would ever be, years spent in the company of men and women who questioned his integrity simply because of his heritage. But he saw honor and integrity in the direct gaze of Kelly Farrell. And then he felt it when she reached out and pressed her palm against the side of his face.

His eyes fell closed for several seconds. He allowed himself the indulgence of savoring the warmth and comfort of her touch. In those silent shared moments, he realized he now possessed an ally, and he felt less alone than he had in many years.

She started to withdraw her hand, but he stopped her by placing his larger one over hers. "Why?" he asked, breaking the silence between them.

"Because I trust you."

He nodded.

"It's time for me to wish you a good night's sleep."

This time, he didn't try to stop her as she moved away from him. He simply watched her as she crossed the room.

She paused, then pivoted to look at him.

"I believe you, Kelly Jennings Farrell."

She exhaled.

He heard the relief in the sound, only then realizing she'd been holding her breath, only then realizing his trust was important to her. Even though he didn't grasp the reason, he sensed they'd forged a meaningful bond.

"Shall we tackle this situation in the morning?" Kelly asked.

Clay inclined his head in agreement. What other choice did he have? "Good night."

She smiled, then slipped out of sight.

Much later, as he made his way from stall to

stall in the barn to check on the horses, Clay reflected on the fact that he had placed his life in the hands of a woman. He realized then that he would never think of one woman in particular as a member of the weaker sex. Kelly Farrell had as much innate strength and courage as any man he'd ever known.

FIVE

Feeling refreshed following an undisturbed night of sleep, Kelly stretched beneath the sheet. She turned her head to confirm the time, but her gaze didn't make it to the digital clock on the night table beside her bed.

Startled to discover she wasn't alone, she sucked in a quick breath and went perfectly still. Awareness rolled over her like crashing waves as she stared at Clay, who stood just a few feet from the edge of her bed. Clad in his buckskins and moccasins, he peered back at her.

Untamed.

Wild.

Seductive.

The words resembled popping corn as they exploded in her head.

His features unrevealing in the diffused morning light, Clay reminded her of a museum-quality sculpture. Kelly knew he was anything but a cold hunk of chiseled stone, however. She'd felt the warmth of his skin, experienced the heat of his passion, and sampled his desire.

Clayton Sloan was very real. More real than any man had a right to be.

Even now, she recalled the feel of his firm lips molded to hers. She also remembered the way he'd thoroughly ravished her senses. Her memories of the night before sent a rush of arousal through her entire body.

She'd felt like an innocent in his embrace, not a woman who'd enjoyed the comfortable intimacy of marriage to a husband she'd loved and respected. Her common sense told her that the absence of physical love for so many years made being touched now that much more profound, especially by a man as stirring as Clay Sloan.

Her body and her emotions clamored for more. Much more.

She wanted Clay, wanted him so much at that moment that she felt unnerved by the desire coursing through her. She fought her feelings, too aware of the cost of poor judgment to allow herself to be guilty of it.

She sat up, pushed her thick auburn hair away from her face, then shoved several pillows behind her back. Because she wore a thigh-length tee and nothing else, she kept a secure grip on the sheet that covered her from waist to toe.

"It is late," he observed, his eyes sweeping

over her sleep-flushed features. "You sleep deeply, like a child."

"My grandmother always told me I slept well because I had a clear conscience."

"She was wise."

Kelly nodded. "Very." She exhaled, the soft, shaken sound doing little, she suspected, to mask the heated flashes of awareness streaking through her veins as she watched him. "Is something wrong? The horses . . ."

He shook his head. "They are well. Groomed and fed."

"All of them?" she asked, her surprise apparent.

A hint of a smile flitted across his hard-featured face. "I could not sleep."

"You must be hungry. I'll start breakfast . . ." Kelly said as she flipped back the sheet.

His gaze briefly dropped to her long, bare legs, then shifted up to her face.

She hastily covered herself again. "If you'll excuse me, I need my robe."

"There is no reason for you to extend yourself on my behalf. I've decided to leave."

Disappointment flooded her. The force of it shocked her. "Is that a good idea?"

"I have no other choice."

"You have a variety of choices, I suspect. We just haven't figured them all out yet. I thought we could do that this morning."

Clay shook his head. "You have enough burdens with a child and this ranch. I do not wish to add to them."

"I appreciate your considerate attitude, but I'm not some hothouse flower who's going to keel over at the first sign of trouble."

He peered at her then, his dark gaze moving over her, slowly, deliberately.

The heat kindling in his eyes amazed her, even made her feel a little reckless. She sensed that he wanted her, too, although she didn't think he would act on the attraction. He was still too wary, too much off balance from his circumstances to behave impulsively.

"What are you thinking?" he asked.

The question caught her by surprise, but it didn't keep her from providing him with an honest reply. "I'm wondering what you see when you look at me."

"A woman."

Amused that such a complicated man would give her such a simplistic answer, she smiled. "Is that all?"

"You are many things." He paused, then sat down on the edge of the mattress. "It would take a man a lifetime to discover them all."

She gripped the sheet even more tightly, more to keep herself from reaching out to touch him than because of any sense of anxiety. Clay Sloan didn't inspire fear. He inspired a rainbow of responses that could easily submerge a woman's common sense, but definitely nothing even remotely resembling fear.

"You understand the need to control your destiny," he observed.

Kelly nodded, shifting to the safety of purely philosophical ground. "It's called being in the driver's seat of one's life. There's always a price, but it's better than being subjugated to someone else's will."

"I agree."

"That's a start." She smoothed her fingertips across the eyelet trim of the sheet.

Clay reached out and snagged her hand. "What I told you last night was the truth."

She nodded. "And I told you I believed you," she reminded him, glad for the physical connection between them. "I still do, even if I don't understand how or why it happened. It's doubtful, though, that others will believe you."

As she studied him, Kelly reflected on her state of mind as she'd fallen asleep the night before. Her imagination had been filled with thoughts of what this man would be like as a lover. Those thoughts were still with her, taunting her composure, threatening the surface appearance of poise she was trying to project.

His fingertips skimmed over the pulse on the inside of her wrist. It sped up. Kelly nearly groaned with embarrassment.

"I *am* from the past," Clay insisted. "My future, as a result, is uncertain."

She believed him, still guided by the same instinct that had prompted her to trust him with Joey. She knew the cynics wouldn't take him at his word. Neither would the authorities. She wondered how the local Cheyenne would react, but her curiosity was short-lived. Thanks to her late husband, she was familiar with the legends and myths that occupied a prominent place in the spiritual side of their culture.

She suppressed a sigh. Clay's future, whatever it might entail, was an unknown quantity. Kelly summoned a reassuring smile as she refocused on him. "Life is filled with uncertainty. Keeps it from getting boring, don't you think?"

"You have many moods," he observed. He moved his thumb in a circular pattern in the palm of her hand.

"Most people do," she answered, somewhat unsettled by his touch and by the fact that he'd shifted the focus of their conversation to her.

He continued to gently stroke her palm. Her skin tingled, and she bit back a sigh. A subtle tremor moved through her entire body, but she managed to conceal her response to him behind an even expression.

"I see a little girl in the woman when I look at you."

Kelly sobered. She'd given up the toys and dreams of childhood long ago. "I'm the keeper of the playyard now."

"You have been lonely since your husband's death."

She saw no point in denying the truth. "Sometimes, but having Joey makes up for the loss."

"He is a good son."

Basking in motherly pride, she couldn't help agreeing with his conclusion about her child. "He's an amazing little boy. I often wonder how I got so lucky."

"It is the boy who is fortunate, Kelly Farrell." Clay fell silent then, his expression reflective.

As they gazed at each other, Kelly didn't press him to speak. She'd learned enough about Clay to realize that he couldn't be rushed and that he liked having the time to form his thoughts before he voiced them.

He exhaled, the sound replete with an array of emotions, some of which she grasped, others that she was reluctant to pursue. He released her hand, and she immediately felt the absence of his warmth.

"I cannot afford the indulgence of childish behavior."

"Which is an excellent reason for you not to make any hasty decisions this morning," she pointed out.

He gave her a sharp look. "You are questioning my judgment?"

"To some degree," she admitted.

"I am not a foolish man," he said, his tone of

voice cooling by several degrees. "I do not behave precipitously when in jeopardy."

Kelly leaned forward. "I think you are quite
intelligent. Too intelligent to walk away from an
ally when you need one." She thought then about
the media's potential reaction to this unusual
man, and she shuddered inwardly at the harm
that could be done to him. "You aren't prepared
for my world, Clayton Sloan. It will shock and
disappoint you. People will try to use you."

"Sand Creek destroyed my faith in the notion
of humanity, so I have no illusions left to shat-
ter."

"Sand Creek?"

"My people . . ." he began, but he didn't
continue. He choked, whatever else he might
have said smothered by the emotion engulfing
him.

She felt the tension that emanated from him
as he fought for control, saw the muscle that
ticked at the top of his jaw. His pain was so palpa-
ble, Kelly felt it in every fiber of her being. She
longed to dispel his negative feelings, but she
knew from personal experience that loss and grief
were a natural part of life.

She suddenly paled, because the puzzle pieces
of his references to Sand Creek and the word
"massacre" finally slipped into place. She'd
taught Colorado history before becoming principal of Holly Grove's grade school. She sought
confirmation of her worst fear as she asked, "You

witnessed the eighteen-sixty-four massacre at Sand Creek, didn't you?"

He met her gaze, his devastation apparent in his expression and posture. "I am a witness to the aftermath. I arrived soon after the slaughter."

"Dear God! Oh Clay, I'm so sorry. I've read accounts of Sand Creek. If it's any consolation, the entire country was outraged by the attack on the Cheyenne by Colonel Chivington and his troops."

"I am outraged," he muttered, his hands repeatedly opening and then closing into fists atop his thighs.

She reached out to him, taking his fists, pushing them open, and sliding her palms across his. She gripped his hands. "It happened a long time ago. There's nothing you can do except mourn the loss and learn from it. That's all any of us can do in the wake of a tragedy."

"For me, it happened yesterday," he reminded her, the starkness of his voice ridding her of any lingering doubts she might have had about him.

Kelly shook her head. "Sand Creek occurred more than a hundred and thirty years ago. Everyone involved is dead and buried, Clay. You cannot change the history of the Cheyenne."

"Can anything be changed?" he demanded, sounding bitter and angry.

"Only one thing," she said gently.

He gave her a cynical look, but he said nothing.

"I'm talking about the future."

"The future does not exist for me."

"How can you possibly know that?"

Jerking his hands free, he surged to his feet. "I know."

"Who elected you God?" she snapped as she pushed aside the covers and slid off the bed to stand before him.

"Be silent, woman!"

"Don't give me orders, dammit. You're a guest in my home, and you shouldn't forget that fact."

"I am leaving."

Like a punctuation mark on his announcement, her alarm clock suddenly buzzed. Kelly flinched, jarred by the sound. Clay froze, unprepared for the sustained wailing. Kelly grabbed the small clock off the night table and silenced it.

Turning to face Clay once again, she explained, "It's just my alarm clock."

"It does not chime," he said through gritted teeth.

"No, it doesn't."

"I do not like your world."

"I don't like it some of the time either, but it's all I've got to work with, so I'm stuck with it."

She placed the clock on the night table and reached for the robe she'd draped across the end of the bed the night before. As she slipped into the garment, Kelly met his gaze.

In spite of Clay's disgruntled expression, he was still the most striking man she'd ever met. His native attire, coupled with his warriorlike demeanor, undeniable physical prowess, and the force of his personality thoroughly seduced her. Again!

To cover her attraction, she cautioned in a firm voice, "You, sir, are also stuck with it."

His frustration with her and the circumstances in which he found himself remained quite evident as he seized her by the shoulders, held her still, and glowered at her. "I reject your evaluation of my current situation."

Unintimidated, she shrugged free of his hold, then ducked out of reach. "Your choice, of course. I don't know about you, but I need a cup of coffee."

Kelly knew she needed a lot more than a jolt of morning caffeine, but she decided not to be greedy. One thing at a time, she reminded herself as she crossed the room and made her way to the landing at the top of the staircase. She said a silent prayer that Clay would follow her.

He did, much to her relief. Kelly made her way down the stairs, through the living room, and into the kitchen. Although she half-expected Clay to keep on walking right out of the house and not give her so much as a backward glance, he surprised her by pausing in the kitchen.

She said very little as he prowled around behind her, watching closely as she made a pot of coffee, placed a coffee cake in the oven to warm it, and set the table. Her sensory awareness of him escalated with every passing second, but she managed to contain her reaction.

It was with a certain amount of relief that she slid into her chair at the table across from him a short while later. His proximity was starting to wear down her defenses.

They ate in silence, but Kelly's appetite flagged after a few bites of food. As she observed Clay, she couldn't help thinking yet again that he was a study in contradictions. Rugged, primitive in certain ways, and possessed of a forceful personality, he also had the most refined manners she'd ever seen and a drawing-room sense of decorum at certain moments that reinforced the unusual life he'd apparently lived.

He was a Cheyenne warrior by birth and a Boston gentleman by training. He was also, Kelly concluded, a man driven by both instinct and intellect. And a lawyer, according to his earlier comments. She couldn't even begin to imagine what it had been like for him to study to be an attorney in the mid-1800s. She suspected he'd encountered all manner of intolerance and bigotry because of his heritage. She sensed that his strength of character had fueled his ability to move between two uniquely different cultures, and she believed that that ability would be his salvation in adapting to life as she knew it.

"You are staring," he pointed out once he neatly refolded his napkin and placed it beside his plate.

She flushed. "You're right, and I apologize. My mind was wandering. I was thinking about what your life must have been like in Boston."

He thought for a moment before responding to her curiosity. "Complicated."

"You have a talent for understatement," she remarked, her tone wry. "Did you like it there?"

"I adjusted. My mother remarried when I was twelve. My stepfather was from Boston. He was a man of wealth and influence in the social and banking communities. They died about six months ago. I settled their estate before I returned to Colorado."

"You hadn't been back to Colorado for a visit in all that time?"

He shook his head.

"How long exactly?"

"Twenty-four years."

In the depths of his eyes, Kelly caught a glimpse of the isolation he'd endured. "How did you deal with the loneliness?"

"At times it was difficult, especially when I was younger—but, as I said, I adjusted."

"You've had an unusual life."

His expression grew contemplative. "It seems that that is my destiny."

"You never married? Never had a family of your own?"

He simply looked at her, the ironic expression on his face his reply.

"I'm sorry," Kelly said quietly.

"I told you I do not appreciate pity."

"I don't pity you, Clay, but I do think you've missed out on a lot of happiness."

"I thought there would be time for a family," he admitted as he leaned back in his chair. "I had hoped . . ." He shook his head, his thick, long hair shifting sensuously across his shoulders.

Kelly's hands itched with the need to touch the dense mane, to feel the silky strands drift through her fingers. "Perhaps there's still time."

"I do not think so."

"You shouldn't give up hope," she urged.

"Now you sound like a child. Wishes rarely come true."

"What did you wish for as a boy?"

"To return to my home and my people, but it was not possible."

"And as a man?"

He hesitated, his inner conflict visible in his dark eyes. "Forgiveness."

Kelly frowned. "Why?"

"Because I knew of the injustices being committed against my people, and I did nothing to stop them."

"You intended to, though, once you returned."

"How do you know that?" he asked, clearly startled by her assumption.

"You're an honorable man."

"You assume a great deal, and you are wrong. There is no honor in what I have done."

"The evidence is before me. I rarely ignore the obvious, Clay."

"Then do not ignore the fact that I must leave this place," he said sharply.

"Where will you go?" she asked, still amazed that he'd judged himself so harshly.

"I will seek answers."

She smiled. She couldn't help her reaction. "You definitely sound like a lawyer." Sobering, she said, "I can help you find some of the answers, but only if you'll trust me."

He gave her a curious look but remained noncommittal.

Kelly sensed that his resistance to the notion she was a viable ally was still very much alive. She told herself his hesitation was based on his experience in another era, but she still resented being grouped with women who had been little more than second-class citizens. That kind of attitude might have worked then, but it was highly impractical in this day and age.

Getting to her feet, she retrieved the coffeepot from the stove and refilled their mugs before taking her seat at the table again.

"Why do you wish to help me?"

"It's the right thing to do," she answered,

aware that she was hedging. She felt guilty the instant the words left her mouth.

The truth of the matter was as obvious as the nose on her face. She didn't want to lose him, despite the bizarre manner in which she'd found him. And she cared about him. More than she probably should, she realized, but she cared nonetheless. As well, she feared he would be harmed or betrayed if left to his own devices.

His gaze narrowed. "That is not an answer."

"Isn't it enough that I want to help you? Is it necessary for me to have a reason or a complicated agenda?"

"It is necessary," he confirmed.

"I think you're a very special man," she said with as much candor as she could muster. "Perhaps in your world you are quite sophisticated, but in mine you're an innocent. I don't like the idea of your being used by people who won't care about your welfare or your feelings."

"I have not known a woman like you."

"Women have changed. We've been liberated."

"Equals," he muttered, his dubious expression revealing what he thought about the concept of gender equality.

"Precisely." Kelly grinned. "Hang in there, Clay Sloan, and we'll bring you up to speed with what's politically correct in no time."

He stiffened. "I do not see the humor in my ignorance of your world."

"It isn't funny. If anything, it's a little sad, but we're going to overcome whatever obstacles we encounter in order to figure out what exactly has happened to you."

"You are sincere." Surprise underscored his words.

"Very sincere," Kelly confirmed. She drained her mug, gathered up her dishes, and walked to the kitchen sink.

Clay followed her, placing his mug on the counter. He paused, his expression filled with confusion as he peered at her.

Kelly felt her heart rate accelerate and her insides start to unravel. She struggled for control. "Thank you," she said, close enough to him to saturate her senses with the scent of his skin.

He smelled of soap and horses and honest sweat. He smelled like what he was—a virile man who evoked emotions and needs she'd thought lost to her forever.

"You're welcome."

When he curved his hand on her shoulder, she held her breath. She wondered if he knew how attracted she was to him.

Clay searched her features, his gaze penetrating. Lifting his hand, he placed it against the side of her face. "You do not regret what passed between us last night?"

"No," she whispered, the warmth of his callused palm and fingers sending spirals of sensation through her. She trembled, but she didn't move away from him. She discovered she lacked the desire, not simply the will.

"Nor do I."

Kelly exhaled, the sound ragged.

"I want you whenever you are near."

She nodded, surprised by his admission. It gave her the courage to speak her own truth. "I feel the same way."

Doubt shone in his eyes. "You have been alone for a long time."

"We've both been alone."

Regret replaced doubt. "I have nothing to offer you."

Just gentleness, integrity, decency, and so many other things she hadn't even begun to discover about him, she thought. He had more to offer a woman than he realized, although this was hardly the time to say the words aloud. He had enough to cope with right now. And so would she, if he remained at the ranch.

"Nothing," he said, repeating the word with a hardness in his voice that made her flinch.

"You're wrong." Changing her mind, she revealed the conviction lodged in her heart and mind. "You have a great deal to offer the right woman. But you're forgetting something."

"I doubt that." He sounded as imperious as a potentate.

Kelly managed not to smile. "I haven't asked anything of you, have I?"

He blinked with surprise. "No, but most women expect—"

"I am not most women," she broke in.

He surveyed her expression. "I think I'm starting to realize that."

She smiled then, reassured that he would at least try not to judge her by standards that didn't apply to her. "Please don't forget it."

"You have my promise, since it is unlikely I will ever forget anything about you."

He drew her into his arms then, embracing her with the kind of gentleness that made her soul ache. She still couldn't quite believe how she felt when he touched her.

Emotion overwhelmed Kelly as she slipped her arms around his waist and rested her cheek against his chest. Tears welled in her eyes as she listened to the fierce pounding of his heart, because she knew they'd reached some kind of pivotal moment in their relationship.

A voice in her head counseled caution and reminded her of the one thing she'd briefly forgotten. Clay might disappear as quickly as he'd appeared in her life. That reality sobered her, and she knew she couldn't ignore it any longer.

Kelly shuddered at the thought of never seeing him again. Extricating herself from his heat and strength, she pressed the palms of her hands against Clay's broad chest. She needed to remain connected to him, but she also needed to see his reaction to what she was about to suggest. Tears welled in her eyes, but she blinked them away.

"Why do you weep?" he asked.

"I don't want . . ." Frustrated with herself, Kelly drew in a steadying breath before she continued. "I don't want anything to happen to you."

Clay appeared amused. "I am able to defend myself. You needn't worry."

She gave him a doubt-filled look. "I know what you're up against. You don't. And I'm also concerned about your potential response to what I'm about to say."

He ran his hands up and down her arms, as if to calm her.

No wonder Bountiful had responded to him, she thought with amazement. He possessed the allure of a shaman, the tactile instincts of a magician.

Clay encouraged, "Speak. I will listen."

"I have a friend, Michael White Horse. He's my late husband's cousin and Joey's godfather. He's one of the few people I trust in this world. Michael is also a member of the local Tribal Council. I think we should talk with him. He will not betray you if you take him into your confidence."

Clay abruptly stepped back from her. "I do not deserve to be among my people."

This wasn't the reaction she'd anticipated. "Of course, you do."

Clay adamantly insisted, "I am not worthy."

"I don't understand."

"Do not press me for an explanation."

She exhaled in frustration. "You're being stubborn again."

Shrugging with false nonchalance, he started to turn away from her.

Kelly caught his arm. "Clay? Wait, please."

"What is it?" he asked, his voice level.

"I'm asking you to trust me."

He smiled, but it was the saddest smile she'd ever seen. "I do trust you, although it surprises me that I am able to."

"Then come with me. We'll speak privately with Michael. He's a very spiritual man, kind and compassionate. Please do this for me, Clay. I won't ask anything else of you."

"I cannot."

Kelly refused to give up. "You must."

Clay pressed his fingertips to his forehead.

"Please," she said softly.

He finally nodded, but with great reluctance.

Kelly didn't understand his attitude, but she didn't waste time trying to figure it out. "I'll call Michael and make an appointment to see him."

"I do trust you, Kelly. You hold my life in your hands," he said before making his way out of the kitchen.

Standing at the kitchen window, she watched him stride across the side yard. He disappeared inside the barn as she dialed a phone number she knew as well as her own. The phone rang several times before it was answered, allowing her the time for a brief prayer that she was doing the right thing for Clay.

SIX

Clay attempted to conceal his uneasiness with the machine Kelly used to transport them to the home of Michael White Horse. At first he sat stiffly in the passenger seat of the vehicle, taking in the terrain around them as they traveled.

Although still rural, the Colorado back country he had once called home had changed dramatically. What he'd learned was an asphalt road reminded him of a black ribbon that wound seemingly without end through the hills and valleys.

Colorful machines of various shapes and colors—what Kelly called *cars*, *trucks*, and *motorcycles*—moved atop the roadway at speeds that startled him at first. After leaving the boundary of the ranch he noticed buildings of every size and description.

Clay viewed Kelly's cluttered world with a

mixture of shock and dismay, but he resolved to keep an open mind. He knew that if the Great Spirit chose to leave him in this time and place, he faced challenges that exceeded his imagination. He couldn't help questioning his ability to adapt to this new life, just as he couldn't help longing for those things with which he was most familiar.

Was it his destiny to remain here? He pondered the question as Kelly slowed the truck and guided it onto a narrow dirt road.

Clay glanced at her. He admired not only the woman, but the manner in which she conducted herself. He allowed his gaze to linger on her profile, reflecting not for the first time on the uniqueness of this woman who seemed to have room in her heart for him. Her inclination to see beyond the barriers that set people apart amazed him.

Her beauty was undeniable, but it was more than a surface image. It reached into her soul. Like his mother, her spirit was gentle and nurturing. Also like his mother, she possessed the nature of a lioness when someone she cared for was in jeopardy.

Outspoken, confident, and poised, she fascinated and intrigued him. He liked her as a person, but he also felt drawn to the passionate woman who had come alive in his arms. Her response to his desire for her surprised him, made his body harden even now as he recalled the depth of her sensuality.

He wanted her, but he'd refrained from taking her. Although his restraint ran counter to his instincts, he had no wish to use her. He sensed he wouldn't be able to dismiss her with the same ease he had employed with a long line of self-absorbed Boston misses who used their bodies to count sexual coups.

He also couldn't forget their differences, despite Kelly's ability to view him without prejudice. She might consider him an equal, but he was a Cheyenne Indian. As well, he was part of a past to which he might be summoned at any moment. Those two realities, he suspected, weren't going to disappear.

"Would you like me to teach you to drive?"

The sound of her voice drew him from his reflective mood. "You are referring to the operation of this machine?"

Flashing a smile in his direction, she nodded.

"It would be the practical thing to do," he conceded.

Her smile evolved into a full-fledged grin. "Something tells me you are an eminently practical man."

He arched a thick black brow, unsure of her meaning. "There is a problem with this trait?"

"Absolutely not," she said. "In fact, it's one of the things I like most about you."

Her soft laughter helped him realize she was

teasing him. He assumed it was her way of trying to ease his trepidation. "I am glad you approve," he answered, a hint of a smile flirting with his lips.

Pulling up in front of a modest frame house a few miles from the main highway, she turned off the engine. "I approve, Clay, of the man and his courage. I shudder to think of what I would do if I found myself in your position."

He shrugged, appreciative of her praise but aware he did not deserve it. He wished he did, though, as much for her sake as his own.

His gaze shifted to the man who walked out onto the porch of the house. He appeared to have reached forty winters. Solidly built and attired in clothing similar to the items Kelly had loaned him, Michael White Horse wore his waist-length hair unbound. His demeanor was that of a man who knew his value and was at peace with himself and his heritage.

As he inspected him, Clay envied Michael White Horse. He felt nothing but inner turmoil.

"You'll like Michael," Kelly said as she pushed open her door.

Clay caught her arm as she reached for her purse. "What did you tell him?"

Settling back against the seat, she covered his hand with her own. "Only that I had a friend who would benefit from his open mind and guidance."

Clay scanned her guileless features. Her smile faded as she peered back at him. He felt her grip tighten on his hand. She shared her strength so effortlessly, he realized.

"Don't worry, please. Michael is a good man."

"He will be your man when you are ready to give Joseph a father?"

Kelly looked startled by his question. "Although I have not had a man in my life since James, Michael isn't a candidate for that role. He's my friend, nothing more." She paused, considering her words for a moment, then admitted, "I haven't wanted anyone until now."

His heart skipped a beat, then two. "Until now?" Clay repeated, taken aback by the possible meaning of her comment.

She spoke softly, sounding oddly breathless. "Until you."

He noticed then the flush that filled her cheeks. Taking her hand, he pressed a light kiss into her palm. "You honor me."

"I think I've just embarrassed myself."

"By being forthright?"

"I'm not usually so blunt," Kelly answered. She seemed to reconsider the statement. "Maybe I am, after all."

"You feel no shame?"

She frowned. "Why would I, Clay?" Comprehension dawned before he could answer her. "My opinions about people, male or female, Indian or otherwise, are based on how they treat me, not on some preconceived notion rooted in ignorance or fear."

Clay appreciated her conviction, but it didn't dispel the anxiety coursing through him. She was one person, and he still felt an absence of confidence in the potential actions and reactions of others. He understood hostility borne out of ignorance, because he'd experienced it firsthand.

His uneasiness persisted, flustering him. He didn't recognize himself like this, and he didn't like himself in this condition. He mustered the appearance of composure for Kelly's benefit. "Whatever happens, I thank you for your help."

She sighed. "You don't owe me thanks. I meant it when I said I cared about you."

Her openness, the absence of artifice and coy little phrases meant to lure and then confuse a man, calmed him as nothing else could have at that moment. He couldn't recall a time in his life when he would have allowed a woman to give him comfort. From Kelly Farrell, however, it was a welcome experience, one he wished to return tenfold to her, he realized. No other woman had ever inspired such feelings in his heart.

"Still trust me?" she asked, lifting her hand to briefly stroke his cheek with her fingertips.

"Yes."

"I'm relieved. You had me worried there for a minute," she told him with a reemerging smile. "Now it's time for you to meet Michael White Horse."

Tugging on the door latch in the same way Kelly had just moments before, Clay released the door and pushed it open. He hesitated once he exited the truck, however. His eyes narrowed as he watched Kelly greet and embrace their host.

Clay fought the urge to wrest her from this man's arms. His common sense told him their contact was innocent and that they were nothing more than friends, but he disliked seeing another man's hands on her.

Shocked to feel jealousy nibbling at the edges of his normally self-contained character, Clay told himself not to think or act like some besotted fool. He also reminded himself that he had no claim on Kelly Jennings Farrell. No claim at all, even though he suddenly felt the urge to stake one that would be clear to all other men.

"How's Joey?" Michael asked as he slid an arm around Kelly's waist and smiled down at her.

"Off for two weeks at Singing Springs Camp with Jenny's kids."

"Enjoy your freedom while it lasts," he counseled. His gaze shifted to Clay, and his smile faded.

She laughed. "Spoken like a man who is singlehandedly raising three teenagers. How are they doing these days?"

"All working summer jobs."

"Good for them."

He shrugged, but fatherly pride glowed in his

dark eyes. "College isn't cheap, and they all want to go."

"You've inspired them," Kelly said.

"I don't know about that, but I'm glad they listen to me when I talk to them."

As the two discussed their children, Clay circled around the front of the truck. Pausing, he scanned the surrounding area, his wariness so instinctive that he didn't bother to conceal it.

A frown on his strong-featured face as his attention kept straying to Kelly's companion, Michael hugged her one last time, released her, and approached Clay. Following introductions made by Kelly, Michael greeted the stranger in Cheyenne, his words and tone formal enough to draw her surprised gaze.

Clay responded with equal formality. He remained where he stood. He watched, his expression neutral, as Kelly made her way to him.

"What is it?" he asked, wondering if she expected to be included in his meeting with Michael White Horse.

It would be best, he had already concluded, for her not to participate in the conversation. The outcome was uncertain from his vantage point. He also knew he had become a complication in her life, and he was reluctant to become a greater cause for worry. He realized now that she fretted over those she cared about if they were troubled.

"I'm going to give you two some privacy,"

she informed him. "I'll be in the garden behind the house."

Clay nodded, grateful he hadn't been placed in a position of offending her. Her notions about men and women being equal in all things still baffled him, although he sensed it was a custom he would have to accept if he lingered in her world.

Kelly took a step closer, close enough for Clay to breathe in her unique fragrance. Desire stabbed at him, his hunger for her spiking unexpectedly as he studied her. He pressed his palms against his thighs to keep himself from reaching out to trace the curve of her cheek. He already knew that her skin felt like the most delicate of rose petals.

He wondered then, as she stood with her back to Michael White Horse and peered up at him, if she grasped the true depth of his longing to know her intimately. He doubted it, just as he doubted his ability to keep it a secret much longer.

Clay glimpsed her concern for him in her large green eyes and troubled expression. It warmed him in unexpected ways. Again he appreciated her sensitivity to his unsettled emotions and her willingness to act as his ally.

The impulse to reassure her came out of nowhere. Trusting his instincts, he acted on it. "You need not worry."

Kelly nodded. "I know, but I can't help myself."

"Please do not," Clay said quietly.

Michael remarked, "I left a basket on the bench in the garden for you, Kelly. The roses are in bloom, if you'd like to gather a bouquet to take home with you."

Turning, she smiled. "Thank you, Michael."

The two men were silent as Kelly made her way along the flagstone path that led to the flower and vegetable gardens behind the house.

Once she disappeared from view, Clay faced Michael White Horse. He silently reminded himself of the fierce and clever nature of the red fox. Revered by all Cheyenne warriors, the fox symbolized the skills needed for conquest and survival in all pursuits. Despite—and, to a certain degree, because of—his years in Boston, he felt a kinship with the animal.

Clay wanted to believe Kelly's assurance that Michael was a wise and kind man. He reserved that judgment as one he would make himself.

Speaking again in the language of their people, Michael White Horse invited Clay into his home.

Clay accepted the invitation, surprised to feel at ease once he entered the dwelling. Bypassing the easy chairs in the main room, the two men sat on a woven native rug in front of a stone fireplace.

Clay began to relax as he looked around. He noticed that Michael White Horse's home was filled with many mementoes and symbols of the

Cheyenne culture. His gaze fell upon an intricately designed shield—a warrior's most prized and sacred possession, which provided him protection against his adversaries. This one had been hung above the mantel.

Atop the mantel rested a lance, decorated with feathers and a banner displaying the legendary red fox. Other items—simple, everyday tools of village life from the past, he noted with some surprise—adorned the tabletops and walls of the parlor.

"You have journeyed far, my brother," Michael observed, again in Cheyenne.

Clay nodded, then described his travels from Boston to Colorado. He proceeded with caution, observing his host's response to his words. The acceptance he saw in Michael's eyes prompted him to reveal more than he had intended.

He found unexpected relief in the chronicling of his tale, and he lost track of the passage of time as they talked. When he reached the part about his travel through time, he hesitated. He studied Michael, wondering exactly how much to reveal.

Despite his initial uncertainty, he sensed that Kelly had been accurate in her judgment of Michael White Horse. He was clearly a man of compassion and deep spirituality, his medicine strong and pure.

Clay wondered, though, if he would judge him a liar if he told him about what he'd discovered at Sand Creek. The images of that day remained fixed in his mind—the carnage, the bodies strewn about, and the stench of death permeating the air.

Desolation filled his spirit as he recalled that day. Drawing in a shattered-sounding breath, he struggled to find the words to describe the tragedy, but they eluded him.

Michael began to speak after a time, his voice subdued but resonant with conviction.

Listening, his shock growing with every passing moment, Clay heard what sounded like reverence in the man's voice as he told of the legend of Cloud Dancer, the grief-stricken warrior who, upon discovering the massacre at Sand Creek, had carried the body of his murdered shaman grandfather into a burning medicine lodge for the journey to the afterlife.

"Why do you tell me of this legend?" Clay asked.

Even as he voiced his question, he weighed Michael's motives for sharing this particular legend. He waited for his response, unable to discern it for himself.

"I have no doubt that you are Cloud Dancer." Michael's voice rang with certainty.

"How can you possibly know this?" Clay pressed.

"I had a vision as a young man. It revealed that you would eventually return to The People when they needed your wisdom."

Clay shook his head. "Although I am called Cloud Dancer, I possess little wisdom."

"Our shamans believe otherwise. I believe otherwise."

"Then you are mistaken," he countered tersely. "I have little to offer anyone, aside from my ignorance of your world."

Michael insisted, "The legend of Cloud Dancer speaks of years of sacrifice, years during which you lived among the whites, became educated in their schools, and adapted to their ways. You became known for your oratory in the courts and for the sharpness of your mind. You were likened to the wily, all-knowing fox. You stood on the field of battle alone. You were tested repeatedly, and you always prevailed. You earned the respect all warriors seek, my brother, and you have much to teach our young ones about the past. The old lessons pave the way to the future. You will be integral to our future."

Humbled and disbelieving, Clay still couldn't relinquish the old image he had of himself. The warrior Michael White Horse spoke of with such eloquence and respect was someone he did not recognize. "I am not deserving of the regard you bestow upon me."

"The warrior known as Cloud Dancer was a man of courage and conviction. In my vision," Michael persisted, "you sought forgiveness for wrongs you did not commit."

"I *cannot* forgive myself. I turned my back on our people."

"Make peace with yourself, Cloud Dancer," Michael urged. "Forgive yourself. Your spirit is being harmed, and this is wrong. Surely you can see this."

"I am not certain I can." After several moments of silence, he asked, "What is your role in all of this?"

Michael smiled for the first time since greeting Kelly earlier that afternoon. "I am to be an ally."

"You accept this?"

"Of course. It is the will of the Great Spirit."

Clay got to his feet and paced the room restlessly.

Michael observed him with a thoughtful expression on his face. "Since you are not ready to walk among The People, will you consider speaking to the Tribal Council?"

"I cannot," Clay insisted.

"I know these men. They are deserving of your trust. They would die rather than betray you."

Coming to a stop, Clay gave him a hard look. "I do not fear betrayal by the Cheyenne."

"I'm glad to hear that, but I still feel you are misguided in your evaluation of yourself."

Clay spoke more sharply than he intended. "*I* will make that determination."

Michael nodded, his regret apparent as he got to his feet. "You are the only one who can."

Clay exhaled, the sound harsh in the quiet of the parlor. "I must have time to consider my destiny. I ask you not to reveal my presence to anyone, not even to the elders who sit on the council."

"If this is your wish, I will respect it. You are welcome to join my household."

Clay resumed his pacing. "Thank you, but no."

"Where will you go?" Michael asked. "How will you live?"

"I am not certain."

Michael hesitated, but only briefly. "Kelly needs help at her ranch. It is a serene place, especially during the summer months."

Clay paused once more. "She possesses a generous heart."

"I have never known anyone quite like her," Michael admitted.

Clay heard the admiration in his voice. Jealousy surged to life inside him. He tamped it down, calling himself a fool in the privacy of his mind. He had no claim on Kelly. He never would.

"Has she told you she runs the Scholarship Committee for the Tribal Council? Her efforts have made it possible for many of our children to attend college."

"I am not surprised." Clay voiced another

thought. "She is not of The People, despite her half-breed son. How is it that she has gained such acceptance?"

"In her heart, I think she is one of us. The elders sense this about her."

Clay pondered Kelly's unique status among the Cheyenne.

"She cares about you," Michael pointed out.

Startled, he flashed a look at his host. "How do you know this?"

Michael smiled. "We're friends, and she's never been one to conceal her feelings. She is an honest woman, perhaps more honest than most."

"I have noticed that characteristic," Clay confessed.

"And others?"

He nodded, certain that Michael White Horse had more to say about her. "She is a beautiful woman," Clay remarked, deliberately opening the door to additional comments.

"Her husband was my cousin. They had a good marriage, but James fell ill and died of cancer soon after Joey was born. She had a difficult time at first, but she recovered from his death."

"I will not make her life more difficult," Clay said, understanding the cautionary words being spoken by Michael White Horse.

Michael chuckled. "Only if that's how she wants it. She is, I'm sure you've discovered, very independent, and she allows her heart to guide her. It's what makes her a wonderful mother, an excellent principal, and an accomplished horse-woman."

"Why does she not have a man?"

"She has not sought one, but that appears to be changing."

Clay inclined his head, but he said nothing. He simply waited, and he was rewarded.

"I've never seen her look at a man in quite the way she looks at you. Not even James, now that I think about it."

"Perhaps you are imagining this."

"I don't think so," Michael said. "I witnessed what passed between the two of you."

"I have no wish to compromise her."

"Then don't, because there are many who would defend her if she is harmed in any way."

"You do not want her for yourself?"

Michael looked amused by the idea. "She isn't a commodity. She's a human being with free will and the right to choose what she wants."

"An equal," Clay observed, the concept still foreign to him. He shot a chagrined look at the man who had welcomed him into his home and was offering him friendship when he needed it most.

Michael laughed, clearly amused that a legend among men felt off balance because of a woman.

After a moment, Clay laughed too.

"Why don't you join Kelly in the garden?" Michael suggested. "I'll be out in a moment."

Clay nodded, suddenly eager to see Kelly. He

wanted the pleasure of her company and the brilliance of her smile. He wanted to stand at her side and bask in her fragrance. He wanted her.

He told himself he would be able to content himself with her companionship and friendship. He suspected that he was lying to himself. How could he find contentment if he didn't claim her as his woman?

SEVEN

Although neither man revealed anything about their lengthy conversation, by the time Clay and Michael rejoined her in the garden, Kelly sensed that a bond had been forged between them. She noticed, too, how much more relaxed Clay seemed, although it was obvious by his subdued demeanor that he still had a great deal on his mind.

She didn't press him for an explanation. Instead, she accepted his reassuring smile as they departed Michael's home and she guided the truck onto the highway for the return trip to her ranch. Once they arrived, Clay thanked her for introducing him to Michael.

Clay also offered to help her with the chores, but she declined, certain that he needed time for himself. He excused himself, indicating that he intended to survey the ranch on foot. She watched him until he faded into the distance on the far side of the pasture, all the while hoping that his sudden restlessness wouldn't result in a permanent departure.

Kelly spent the next few hours in the barn, attending to the horses. She saved Bountiful for last. Relieved to discover that the animal seemed calmer and more receptive to her presence, she knew she had Clay to thank. She reminded herself to acknowledge his help with the filly.

Walking back up to the house late in the afternoon, she retrieved several shirts and two pairs of jeans from the bureau in which her brother stored some of his clothes. She placed them on a bench near the kitchen door, so she would remember to give them to Clay. He couldn't, she reasoned, wear the same clothes day in and day out, whether he remained at the ranch or not.

She hoped he would stay on, but she feared she was indulging in wishful thinking. After all, Clay hadn't made a secret of his intentions. He planned to leave—to seek answers, as he'd put it. She knew it was just a matter of time before he did. That realization made her feel empty and sad inside.

As she fried chicken and made potato salad for the evening meal, Kelly tried to concentrate on the tasks at hand, but her thoughts repeatedly strayed to Clay. He was unlike any other man she'd known, regardless of the fact that he was from a past she could only imagine with the help of history books. Measured against any man from any era she might select, she knew in her heart he was unique.

Cleaning up the kitchen, she relived the moments of intimacy they'd shared. Her senses provided her with a refresher course on the emotions he'd awakened within her and the erotic feelings he'd evoked in her body.

A soft sound of longing escaped her as she stood at the sink. The pan she held slipped from her fingers and plopped into the soapy water. Slumping against the counter's edge, she closed her eyes and tried to compose herself, but the effort proved futile.

Kelly had never felt such overwhelming hunger for a man, and for a moment the consuming quality of that hunger unnerved her. She wasn't accustomed to such forceful feelings or of being so captivated by a man that she couldn't get him out of her mind.

A woman who prided herself on her self-control and clear-headed thinking, she was at a loss to explain why a complete stranger had the power to move her in ways that her late husband had not. She didn't feel guilty—just confused.

She knew Clay desired her. She'd seen it in his eyes, experienced it in his touch.

Was desire enough? Kelly wondered, thinking of the years she'd spent alone. Should she simply go with the moment and her feelings?

Could she surrender to primitive instincts just this once?

A part of her wanted to, but another part of her insisted that only a fool dove headlong into the unknown.

As she searched her conscience and her heart for answers she could live with, Kelly heard the kitchen door slam. Startled, she straightened. Her gaze collided with the object of her conflicted thoughts and emotions.

Clay paused a few steps from her position at the sink.

Kelly felt a flush heat her cheeks. She looked away, embarrassed to be caught fantasizing, mortified because she felt certain her thoughts would be readily apparent to an observant man like Clay Sloan.

"Something smells good," he commented by way of a greeting.

Meeting his eyes, Kelly opened her mouth to speak, then snapped it shut. What could she say to him? *I don't want food—I want you.* Hardly the words of a grade school principal, she cautioned herself.

She exhaled, the sound so shaken that it drew an immediate frown from Clay. She saw his mouth move, knew he was speaking to her, but an odd roaring in her ears prevented her from hearing him.

He approached her, very slowly. "You are ill?" he asked.

She shook her head. Not ill, she thought. Just suffering from sensory overload anytime you're within range.

"What is it?" he pressed, his hand moving to her shoulder.

The protectiveness of the gesture and the concern in his expression made her want to weep. How long had it been since a man had cared enough about her to voice his concern about her well-being? Unfortunately, she knew the answer: too long.

"Kelly?"

"I . . ." She shook her head. "Nothing."

She reached for the dish towel she'd left on the counter and dried her hands. She needed to put some space between them, needed to calm down and reclaim the dignity she'd guarded with unflagging vigilance her entire life.

She might have been able to follow through on her good intentions if he'd remained near the door, but he was too close to ignore. Much too close. Picking up the woodsy scent of his very male body, she inhaled sharply. She stepped back in self-defense, but he caught her arm.

"What's wrong? Has something happened to Joseph?"

"Nothing's wrong," she insisted. "Joey's fine. Everything's fine."

His hand drifted down her arm, his touch gentle.

Kelly suddenly grasped the extent of his influence over Bountiful. She trembled, her imagination going wild and images too erotic for words filling her head.

Stiffening, he withdrew his hand. He looked cool and aloof. He also looked angry. "If you would like me to leave you alone, I will."

"No, don't leave. I'm fine. Really." *Liar*, her conscience asserted.

Some of the rigidness left his body. "I want to believe you, Kelly, but it's difficult given your agitated state."

"I'm not agitated. I don't *get* agitated," she insisted. Tears brimmed in her eyes. Kelly felt like a fool as she blinked them away.

He reached out to her again, gently turned her so that she faced him, and curved his hands over her shoulders. "Have I caused your distress?"

She shook her head, her gaze captured by the pulse beating in the hollow of his throat. "No," she whispered, trembling anew thanks to her struggle not to fling herself into his arms. "It's me. I'm just having an off day, I guess."

He nudged her face up with his fingertips so that he could see her expression. She knew he glimpsed the longing and need she felt, knew it the instant she saw the change in his eyes. As black as a starless night sky, they glowed with an awareness that eclipsed anything she'd ever seen in a man's eyes when he looked at her.

She almost moaned aloud her amazement,

but she managed to smother the urge and the sound.

He wanted her.

She wanted him.

Why couldn't she have what she wanted? Why couldn't life be simple? she wondered, although she knew it wasn't and never would be.

She forced herself to speak. "Clay, I . . ."

"Yes?"

"I need . . ." *You*, she nearly said. ". . . to sit down. I'm tired." Feeble, she thought in disgust. Truly feeble.

Instead of taking her at her word, he drew her closer, ever so slowly. It was as if he understood what she'd wanted to say but didn't have the courage to admit. As if he wanted the very same thing.

Feeling as though she were moving in slow motion, Kelly welcomed the contact with his body when it finally happened. She melted into him, feeling vaguely boneless. Through the cotton of his shirt she absorbed the heat of his muscular body, felt the heavy thudding of his heart.

She shuddered, and a heavy sigh of relief spilled past her lips. She wanted to crawl into him and never leave. She wanted so much from him in those next few moments that she didn't even know how to describe it all. She felt submerged in desire. It flowed hotly through her veins, stunning her with its intensity and force.

"Talk to me," he urged as he held her. His large hands moved up and down her back.

She felt soothed and stimulated, all at the same time. She wondered if he realized the impact he was having on her—wondered, as well, if he grasped the true depth of her need and that it threatened to turn her world upside down. Her silence persisted. She simply couldn't think of anything rational to say.

"Please share your thoughts," he encouraged.

Kelly finally lifted her face, her gaze scanning his features, her fingers kneading the base of his spine, although she didn't even realize what she was doing until she felt the change taking place in his lower body. Her eyes widened, and she sucked in a startled breath.

Clay shifted against her, tantalizing her even more with the hardness of his loins and the subsequent shudder that rocked his entire body. He groaned, the sound coming from deep inside him.

The sound also reached into her soul, setting it aflame.

Raising one of his hands, he traced the width of her lower lip with his thumb while his gaze roved over her heart-shaped face. "You tempt me," he whispered.

Her eyes fell closed, her wits fleeing to some distant place, her awareness of the world reduced to the sensations caused by his touch and the power contained in his tense body. Kelly exhaled, the gush of air so rich with unvoiced desire that it penetrated her dazed consciousness.

"You are an extraordinary woman," he said, his tone raw and revealing.

Kelly blinked with surprise. Oddly enough, his words helped steady her. She knew then that he, too, grappled with the unexpected attraction between them. She didn't feel so foolish, nor so alone.

He edged backward, although he didn't release her completely. Clasping her wrists, he raised her hands and pressed a kiss into each palm.

Stunned, she held her breath and watched him. She silently marveled over the denseness of his eyelashes, the slashing thickness of his brows, and the character evident in his angular face. The latter, a composition of strong lines and hollows, spoke of his heritage and life experiences in ways both obvious and subtle.

Clay cupped her face with his hands. "We must talk."

"I know," she breathed.

"There is much to discuss."

She nodded. She agreed with him, but was she ready for this particular discussion? She seriously doubted it.

He stepped away from her. Reaching a spot in the center of the spacious kitchen, he turned and looked at her.

She remembered the meal she'd prepared

only because she noticed the platter of fried chicken she'd placed on the table a little while earlier. Suddenly unnerved by the intensity of his expression, Kelly said the first thing that popped into her head. "Dinner's almost ready. Why don't we talk during our meal?"

Clay looked startled, then mildly amused. "That is not the discussion I had in mind."

Too skittish to cooperate with his polite statement, she sidestepped his real meaning. She wasn't ready for a nuts-and-bolts conversation about their attraction to each other. She had to find her common sense first, not to mention her self-control.

She kept her voice firm and even. "If you'll help me set the table, I'll serve our meal."

"Equality in all things?" Clay confirmed, laughter dancing in his eyes—eyes that just moments earlier had reminded her of glowing embers in a fireplace.

"Exactly."

"I understand."

"Good," she brightly chirped, determined to get things back to normal in a hurry.

They worked together in the next few minutes. Kelly found unexpected pleasure in sharing the simple tasks, then promptly told herself she'd probably enjoy digging ditches with this man.

I've finally lost my mind, she thought as she took her seat at the table and reached for her napkin.

They ate in relative silence, save for the usual requests for salt, pepper, and butter. Kelly finally started to relax as they neared the end of their meal. Once she served dessert, bowls of fresh strawberries and cream and mugs of coffee, she felt fortified and more confident of her ability to carry on a coherent conversation with Clay. She knew him well enough now to realize he would pursue the topic he'd raised a little earlier.

After sampling the strawberries, Clay remarked, "Your judgment regarding Michael White Horse was accurate. He is a thoughtful and wise man, and I have a great deal to think about as a result of our conversation."

"He's been a good friend over the years, especially since James died."

"He spoke to me of your late husband."

Kelly took a sip of coffee. "I'm not surprised. They were very close friends, not just cousins."

"Like brothers," Clay said.

She smiled. She understood the cultural traditions that fueled his assumption that friendship turned men into brothers. In the case of James and Michael, it happened to have been true. "Very much like brothers," she confirmed.

"He urged me not to leave this place in haste."

"And do you intend to take his advice?" Her heart picked up speed as she waited for his answer.

"I think it's the best course of action for now."

She carefully placed her spoon beside her half-eaten bowl of strawberries. Settling back in her chair, Kelly made a concerted effort to project a calm she didn't actually feel. "What are your plans?" she asked.

"I've decided to seek employment. It will take me time to determine my true destiny."

She closed her hand around the napkin beside her coffee mug.

His gaze dipped to her white-knuckled grip on the fabric. "Is there a problem?"

She shook her head, released the wadded up material, and tucked her hands into her lap. "I thought you'd leave."

"Is that what you wish me to do?"

"Of course not."

"Does it matter if—" he began.

She broke in, unable, unwilling to stop herself. "It matters, Clay. *You* matter."

His gaze speculative, he voiced the obvious question. "Why?"

"I'd miss you," Kelly answered, very aware of precisely what she was admitting.

"You do not know me well enough to feel my absence."

"I want to know you. And you're wrong. I would feel your absence. I would feel it deeply." She spoke so softly that she wondered if he even heard the words—wondered, that is, until she saw what appeared to be relief in his remarkable black eyes.

"I would miss you too," Clay said. "Very much, I think."

She stared at him, then pulled herself back to reality by the sheer force of her will. "What kind of employment would suit you?"

Kelly knew all too well that the job as her hired man was a far cry from his usual pursuits. She doubted he would want to take such a step down in status or pay, but she kept her fingers crossed anyway. Clay's talent with horses was undeniable, and she needed that talent with a full stable that summer. She needed it almost, she realized in a flash of total honesty with herself, as much as she needed him.

"I wish to apply for the position of hired man, if that is acceptable to you."

"It's more than acceptable, but I can't pay you a great deal of money," she cautioned, thrilled that he was even interested in the job.

He shrugged. "What you deem appropriate is what I will accept."

"You're a lawyer, Clay."

"Only in my time. For now, I am simply a man who wishes to work for as long as . . ." He hesitated, obviously considering how to proceed. ". . . for as long as I am here."

She nodded, his reminder that no one could predict the length of his stay both sobering and unnecessary. Life for Clayton Sloan was a one-day-at-a-time proposition, and she knew that neither one of them was in danger of forgetting that fact.

Her practical side much in evidence, Kelly itemized the responsibilities of the job. She also told him the salary he could expect to receive each week.

He voiced his surprise. "That is an impressive sum."

"Sadly, it's not. At least not when compared to the wages most people expect to earn these days. Once you've gone shopping with me, you'll have a clearer idea of what I'm talking about. Meals and lodging come with the job, though— and, of course, a very curious little boy who rarely stops talking."

"You are an excellent cook."

"So my son tells me."

"He is wise beyond his years." His solemn-sounding remark was at odds with the humor in his eyes.

She laughed. "He's a wiseacre most of the time, but he's all mine."

"I will begin in the morning," he informed her, sounding like the boss and not the employee.

Kelly blotted her lips with her napkin to conceal her amusement. Clay Sloan would never be anyone's *hired man*. He was very much his own man, even if he had to earn a living like other mortals.

She voiced a question that had occurred to her several times since their departure from Michael's home. "Did Michael suggest that you meet with the Tribal Council?"

Clay nodded, his features growing tight as he peered back at her.

"I take it by your silence that you aren't willing to speak to them yet."

"I may never be ready, but it is a decision I will make when the time is right. I will not be rushed."

"No one's going to try and force you to do anything you don't want to do, especially not me. Nor Michael, for that matter. He isn't the kind of person who indulges in manipulation."

"That was my conclusion, as well. I believe he will honor his pledge to keep my presence in this time a secret." Clay drank the last of his coffee and set aside his mug. "He spoke to me of a legend."

"The Cheyenne culture is rich with legends and myths," Kelly said. "James often shared them with me, especially on cold winter nights in front of the fireplace."

"Do you believe in them?"

"More often than not. They remind me of morality plays. In fact, I've used them as a teaching tool."

He nodded, looking reflective. "That is a good way to describe them."

"Had you heard this particular legend before, or was it something new?" she asked.

"I hadn't heard it before. It was a tale about a warrior and what he did when he discovered the massacre at Sand Creek."

"And what exactly did he do?" she asked, sensing by his tone and expression that his reply was important.

"He carried the dead body of his grandfather, a holy man among the Cheyenne, into a burning medicine lodge for the journey to the afterlife."

She knew the identity of the warrior without asking. She saw the truth in Clay's pain-filled eyes. She was amazed he'd brought up the subject in the first place. He was an intensely private man.

"The warrior was called Cloud Dancer."

"The warrior was you," she said quietly. "You must have been shocked." *I am*, she realized, trying not to overreact.

"I was. I still am. Someone must have survived."

"There are ways to find out," she reminded him. "We could start at the library. If that doesn't work, we can speak to the Cheyenne historians at the university if you prefer to avoid the elders who sit on the Tribal Council."

He nodded thoughtfully as he studied her. "You can be very logical at times."

Brought up short by his apparent surprise that she possessed the trait, she shook her head in dismay. He had a lot to learn. She couldn't help wondering if there would be enough time.

"Equality?" he confirmed.

"That, and the fact that I taught history."

"I understand."

Her voice as crisp as a fall morning in the mountains, she replied, "I doubt it, but I'm optimistic about your potential as long as you keep an open mind." Kelly turned her attention back to the original topic of conversation. "Was the legend accurate? Did you carry your grandfather into a burning medicine lodge?"

"Yes," he admitted, closing his hands into fists atop the table. "It is my last memory of my time."

She didn't miss the shift in his mood. She realized then that he had sought death in his grief. "I'm not sure what to say to you."

He drilled her with a hard look. "There is nothing to say."

"I know!" she flared, her emotions shooting to the surface and overtaking her self-control.

"You are becoming distressed again. Does this happen often?"

"Don't be so bloody analytical," she snapped, suddenly furious with him for exercising such ruthless control over his emotions. "Of course, I'm distressed! You've been through your own personal version of hell on earth, and you're still able to talk about it. That's nothing short of a miracle."

"You have suffered losses," he reminded her, "and you speak of them."

"You're comparing apples to oranges, Clay. We're talking about an entire village. Scores of people, perhaps hundreds."

He surged to his feet, his voice like ice as he reminded her, "I know exactly what we're talking about. I was there."

Abandoning her chair, Kelly followed him. "Clay, I want to help you, but I don't know how."

He stopped abruptly and turned to face her. "Sometimes nothing helps. Certain kinds of pain are a part of life and living. You know this as well as I do."

She nodded, her shoulders slumping as she stood before him.

Lifting his hand, he trailed his fingertips across her cheek. "My destiny can be revealed only by the Great Spirit. It is in His hands. It is also preordained. I cannot change it. You cannot change it either. No more than you can change the fact that Joseph's father died while he was an infant. You cannot fix everything, Kelly Farrell, although you appear inclined to try."

He sounded just like James, she realized. Her husband had comforted her as he lay dying when she discovered that the force of her will wasn't enough to cure him of the cancer that had taken him in a matter of a few months.

"Tell me something I haven't already figured

out," she challenged, her green eyes sparkling with frustration.

Clay gathered her into his arms a moment later, as though he understood that she needed closeness far more than words of reassurance.

EIGHT

Ten days later, Clay closed the rear gate of the truck after loading the few supplies left over from repairs on the pasture fence. Peeling off the leather gloves he wore, he threw them in the back of the truck. He lifted his arms, stretching the kinks from his muscular body.

His years as a lawyer, combined with an estate replete with servants, had eliminated the need for true physical labor. Aside from riding early each morning, he'd spent most of his time in his office or in the courtrooms of Boston and Washington.

Bare-chested, his long hair pulled back from his face and loosely braided, and clad in jeans and moccasins, Clay savored the gentle breeze wafting down from the surrounding mountain peaks and flowing over his body. He couldn't recall a time when working with his hands had been more satisfying. He felt his spirit and body mending themselves, although he was still no closer to the answers he sought. He credited Kelly for the good feelings he now enjoyed. Her gentleness and acceptance were like a healing balm.

"Those fenceline repairs would have taken me two or three weeks if I'd done them alone," Kelly remarked as she retrieved a large cooler from the front seat of the truck. "It's a relief to have help."

Clay nodded as he wiped the sweat from his face with the bandanna he kept knotted at his throat. "This is man's work. You shouldn't even be out here."

"This is the work of the person or persons responsible for the care and maintenance of a small ranch," she reminded him, the smile on her face softening her rebuke.

He inclined his head, a hint of an answering smile tugging at his lips. "I stand corrected."

He was glad, though, that she didn't object when he relieved her of the heavy cooler and carried it to a shady spot beneath an ancient maple tree at the edge of the pasture. He was willing to embrace the concept of gender equality, but he couldn't and wouldn't ignore the manners ingrained in him while still a young man.

"Why did your hired man leave?" he asked.

He watched her shake out the blanket she'd brought and then kneel down atop it. Clay stretched out on his side opposite her. She handed him a thermos of lemonade and two plastic cups before she answered him.

"I fired Martin when I caught him mistreating one of the horses. He actually expected me to write a letter of reference for him, but I refused. He's lucky I didn't call the sheriff and file charges against him for animal abuse."

Clay poured lemonade into the cups, placed one on a level spot atop the blanket for Kelly, and drained the other one before refilling it. "You showed excellent judgment."

She handed him a plate and a napkin. "I thought so."

Under Clay's observant gaze, Kelly opened several containers and placed them in the center of the blanket like a buffet. He noted the economical efficiency of her movements, but he also noticed the way she nibbled on her lower lip when she was concentrating on a task. The latter habit never ceased to amuse him.

"Help yourself," she encouraged as she reached for her lemonade. "We have ham-and-cheese sandwiches, fruit salad, potato chips, and an assortment of Jenny's prizewinning pickles."

"A veritable banquet."

She grinned. "Just lunch."

"Accept the compliment," he instructed.

Pursing her lips, she pondered his order. "All right," she decided a few moments later.

"I like a biddable woman."

"You're in trouble then, because I'd never

pass the entrance test to that little club. In fact, I don't think I've ever met a biddable woman."

"Another reason for gender wars?" he asked, summoning from his memory a phrase she'd used.

Kelly laughed. "Probably, but they're mostly just periodic skirmishes these days."

Clay chuckled, then directed his attention to the food spread out before him. He'd already concluded that the mating rituals between men and women hadn't really changed since his time, although many of the rules of acceptable behavior apparently had.

Clay appreciated the comfortable silence that settled around them as they ate their lunch. He appreciated the simplicity of a day spent working outdoors. And he particularly appreciated the woman seated across from him.

Sensitive, witty, intelligent, and deeply passionate about the people and things that were important to her, she possessed qualities that fascinated him.

He now viewed her strength of character and sense of purpose as assets, not in the least unfeminine. Although she would have been considered shockingly outspoken in his time, he valued her honesty and her ability to confront any issue that concerned her.

He'd even come to terms with her attire, although it still aroused him to see her form so explicitly displayed by snug-fitting jeans and soft cotton shirts that outlined the fullness of her breasts and her tiny waist.

He saw glimpses of her vulnerable side at odd moments, as when he caught her studying him, but he refrained from questioning her about her thoughts. He sensed that they resembled his, although she appeared uneasy at the prospect of actually revealing her feelings.

He respected her privacy, just as Kelly respected his, but he felt the underlying tension of the restraint she practiced. He knew the cost of his own restraint, having spent several restless nights dealing with the desire she inspired.

As he watched her now, he again quelled the urge to draw her into his arms and hold her. Not touching her during the last ten days had been pure agony, but he'd managed to keep his promise to himself that he wouldn't compromise or dishonor her. She was the kind of woman a man didn't trifle with—the kind of woman meant for commitment and safekeeping.

Clay exhaled, the sound ragged enough to draw Kelly's gaze. To cover the stirrings taking place in his body, he pushed to his feet and turned away from her. "I'm going to walk for a short while," he announced.

She nodded, clearly bewildered by his abruptness. "Enjoy yourself."

He set off without further comment, his pace brisk as he put as much distance between them as he could for the time being. His entire body ached, and he wanted her with an intensity that threatened his ingrained sense of right and wrong.

As he walked, Clay found little of the relief he sought. Kelly tempted him. Tempted him with the sound of her laughter, her quick mind, the gentleness of her touch, and his memory of her taste when he'd kissed her.

He recalled her response. Like an exploding powder keg, she'd matched him in hunger while simultaneously inflaming his senses and tantalizing his imagination. He longed to have her naked so he could explore every fragrant curve and hollow of her hourglass-shaped body. He wanted to bury himself in her sweetness and heat, wanted to linger within her until they were both so spent with satisfaction that the world and their differences ceased to matter.

He wanted those things and more as he imagined their bodies joined in passion. The images in his mind brought a groan of near-pain to his lips, and he called himself a fool for indulging in such self-torment. He walked on, his expression determined, his insides throbbing with unfulfilled impulses. Impulses he'd always had the power to control in the past. Impulses that now made a mockery of his traditionally reserved manner.

The pond at the far end of the pasture beckoned.

Standing at the edge of the water a few moments later, Clay stepped out of his moccasins and stripped off his jeans. As he walked into the cold water, a shiver ripped through him, but he welcomed the shock to his body as a much-needed distraction from the pulse-pounding desire that threatened his self-control and common sense.

He eventually left the pond, allowed the sun to dry him, and then reclothed himself. As he made his way back to the site of their picnic lunch, he felt more in control of himself.

Clay silently vowed to stay that way.

Had Kelly not chosen to stretch out atop their blanket and take a nap after repacking the cooler, he told himself he might have been able to keep his vow.

Sprawled on her back and a hint of a smile on her lips, she personified all things innocent and seductive.

Clay towered over her, his hands clenched at his sides, his heart racing, his loins swelling, thanks to the heat surging recklessly through his veins. He dropped down beside her, telling himself he could hold her close and do nothing else. He needed to believe that lie.

He gathered her into his arms, stunned when she instinctively burrowed against his bare chest in her sleep and then looped an arm around his neck. He heard, then felt, the sigh that escaped her when it flowed warmly across his skin. Her trust was like an indictment; he told himself yet again that he would simply hold her close while she slept.

She stirred in his embrace a little while later.

His body already hard and tight with tension, Clay waited for her to reclaim her awareness of herself and her surroundings.

She smiled sleepily as she looked up at him. "I guess I was more tired than I realized."

"That's what happens when you do men's work."

"You're impossible."

"Just surveying the evidence before me."

She laughed. "Ever the lawyer."

The alluring sound of her laughter and the seductive feel of her body aligned with his sent his senses into overdrive. His body reacted to her and his need of her. He fought for control, but Kelly thwarted him without realizing it when she shifted against him.

She froze, her startled gaze flying to his face. "Sorry," she mumbled as she started to ease free of him.

He stopped her. "There is a discussion we've been avoiding."

"I know."

"It is past time to talk about what's happening between us."

She nodded. "You're right, but maybe we should wait until we're sitting or standing."

Shocked for a brief moment, he peered at her in disbelief. Then he laughed ruefully, in spite of the fierce tightening of his body. Desire throbbed like a primitive drumbeat inside him, echoing in his heart and soul. He wondered if he would ever not hear the sound and connect it to Kelly.

"What's so funny?" she asked.

The expression on her face assured him she was somewhat hesitant to hear his reply. Reaching up, he caressed her cheek with his fingertips, his gaze scanning her flushed features.

"Clay, tell me what's so funny," she insisted.

He reluctantly withdrew his hand. "You. Me." He shrugged, although he didn't feel any of the casualness the gesture conveyed. "Us?"

"Am I supposed to pick one?" she asked, squirming suddenly. The welcoming cradle of her hips came into contact with his loins.

Biting back a groan, he caught her hip with a restraining hand. "Kelly," he said, a clear warning in his voice.

"There's a rock underneath me." She twisted against him yet again.

Releasing her, he rolled onto his back, closed his eyes, and dragged in several uneven breaths.

Kelly sat up, tugging her T-shirt into place. "I'm really sor . . ."

"Give me a minute," he cut in, trying not to sound as though he'd just emerged from some medieval torture chamber.

She leaned over him, her auburn hair framing her face with a halo of heat-induced curls that had worked free of the casual topknot she'd fashioned earlier in the day.

He watched her through half-lowered lids. Watched her and wondered what she was thinking and feeling. She looked flushed and rumpled and far too inviting, but also very thoughtful as she studied him.

"You have the most beautiful hair," she said softly.

It was the last thing he had expected her to say, and he just stared at her.

"May I touch it?" she asked.

He nodded, still somewhat taken aback by her request. "Of course."

She unbraided the thick strands and threaded her fingers through, her expression one of total fascination as she fingercombed a section of the waist-length black mane. "It's like silk." She let the strands drift through her fingers before she glanced at him. "I thought it would be."

His black eyes narrowed to slits; his entire body was seized by a fine trembling. He could barely think, let alone reason with his usual clarity.

"I've been told that a warrior's hair is one of the most important symbols of his prowess as a man."

"Something like that," he managed, his heart galloping like a prize racehorse.

Her unique fragrance filled his senses each time he took a breath. Combined with the soft sound of her voice and the gentleness of her touch, the impact on him was complete. And devastating.

She smiled at him. "I can see why."

"Your touch is gentle."

"I could say the same thing about you. You've worked wonders with Bountiful."

"And seductive," he added, curious how she would react to this additional observation.

She looked away.

He gently nudged her chin with his knuckles so that he could see her face. "No comment?" he asked.

"You seduce with your touch as well."

"Are we still talking about Bountiful?"

She shook her head. "No," she admitted, her green eyes like the finest polished jade, her breathing sounding faintly shallow.

He sensed that she had more to say. "What else?"

"We're also talking about me."

After considering his options, Clay selected the direct approach. "Does it bother you to want me? Does it trouble you that I want you just as much?"

"I'm bothered—more *bothered* than I ever have been by a man—but I'm not at all troubled, because I've stopped fighting my feelings."

He went very still inside, his heart stuttering to a brief stop as he grappled with his shock. "When did this happen?"

"A few days ago."

"Why did it happen?" He wanted no confusion between them, no remorse or regret or recriminations.

"I think it was destined to happen," she said with characteristic openness. "I'd be dishonest if I pretended I don't care about you or that I haven't thought about what you would be like as a lover. And I will not pretend that I don't want you." Kelly studied him. "Have I shocked you?"

"I appreciate your candor, and yes, you've shocked me," he admitted, taking her hands and joining them to his so their fingers formed a loose weave.

"Am I terribly forward by the standards of your world?"

He chuckled. "Remarkably so, but I approve."

"Would you have me play coquettish games with you, Clay? I wouldn't really know where or how to start, if that's what you expect of me. I've always secretly loathed game-playing between a man and a woman."

"I would be saddened if you behaved in this manner." Amazed yet again by this uncommon woman, he silently thanked the Great Spirit for bringing her into his life during this troubling time.

He then told Kelly of the kind of love games he wanted to share with her, the words slipping past his lips in French, the language of lovers throughout the ages and taught to him by an exotic courtesan he'd encountered in Paris after completing his studies at Harvard.

Kelly responded to his vivid description of the ways in which he dreamed of making love to her, her voice low and rich with her innate sensuality. She spoke to him in the same language, revealing her desire to know him intimately in every way a woman can know a man, then laughingly apologized to him in English for her halting use of high school and college French.

"No apologies are required." He gathered her into his arms. "You tempt me beyond reason. You have since the first moment I saw you."

She moved eagerly into his embrace, her slender legs twining around his more muscular ones once he shifted onto his side.

He shuddered as she pressed against him.

"No more than you tempt me," she belatedly confessed as she circled his neck with her arms and gazed at him.

Her honesty was more tantalizing than anything he'd ever experienced with a woman, although it came as no real surprise to him. He already knew she was a woman who honored her nature. She was real, and she possessed a purity of heart and spirit that had the power to humble him.

Clay absorbed the feel of her from chest to toes just seconds before he claimed her lips. Her lips parted in the next instant, and their mouths fused.

He tasted her relief and her hunger a split second later, aware that she tasted the same things in his kiss. He felt the tremor that rocked through her shapely body, felt, as well, her full breasts as they plumped against the hard wall of his chest.

His embrace tightened as he lost himself in the flavors and textures of her passion. No longer anyone other than an honest man who wanted his woman, he surrendered to the inevitability that it was their destiny to become lovers.

Where this merging of bodies would lead them, he didn't know. The world, past, present, and future, faded to the periphery of his consciousness. It disappeared altogether when Kelly angled her head and deepened their kiss even more.

She drove her fingers into his thick hair, kneading his scalp with her fingertips and purring low in her throat like a feline who'd finally found her mate. She explored the heat of his mouth with curious, darting swipes of her tongue before sucking at his. She rocked against him, her pelvis stroking the ridge of hard flesh still contained by his jeans.

Feeling almost feverish, Clay shifted her onto her back without ending their kiss. Resting the weight of his upper body on his elbows, he lodged his aching loins in the cradle of her thighs, his body driven by instinct and need as he surged against her. He saturated his senses with her taste, the fragrance of her skin, and the luxurious softness of her feminine curves as he plundered her mouth.

She skimmed her fingers down the sides of his neck, across his broad shoulders, and then over the width of his muscular chest. As she trailed her fingertips over the sculpted muscle of his upper body, she stoked the flames burning within him to a dangerous level.

Clay tugged her shirt free and pushed it above her breasts. Kelly finished the job when she jerked it up and over her head, then cast it aside. The abbreviated chemise she wore confused him, and his eyes revealed his uncertainty with the garment.

Kelly released the catch at the front of her bra, but she stopped there, invitation and a hint of a challenge in her expressive eyes as she watched him.

Clay peeled the fabric away from her breasts, then filled his hands with the mauve-tipped globes. She shuddered, her back arching and a sharp breath hissing past her lips. She moaned his name.

He watched her then, savoring the breathless sighs he provoked as he caressed her breasts and then tugged at her nipples until they reminded him of tiny daggers. Leaning down, he sucked a taut tip between his lips, teething it with care while also gently twisting her other nipple with his fingers. She trembled, her fingers digging into his back as she clung to him and her lower body moving restlessly until his loins ached from the stimulation.

He shifted his attention to her other breast, suckling her sensitive flesh, then teething, then suckling again. He heard his name spill past her lips yet again, and he felt the escalating tension that made her writhe beneath him. She grew more and more volatile with every passing second.

Lifting his head, he saw the glazed look in her eyes. His own body quaked with the need for release thanks to her uninhibited sensuality.

"I want to feel you inside me," she whispered.

Her words resonated within him like the aftermath of a cannon blast. Clay sat back on his haunches, freed the buttons of her jeans before stripping them, along with a skimpy lace confection, from her trembling body. Skimming his palms up the length of her long legs, he fought for control.

He also gave Kelly time to voice any second thoughts she might have. He wanted her to be certain about their joining, although he longed to abandon his caution and simply bury himself in her heated softness before he took his next breath.

Kelly sat up, then got to her feet. She stood before him. Naked. Gloriously naked. She was more perfectly formed than he'd imagined, more of a natural seductress than any woman had a right to be. And she was giving herself to him, he realized, his heart filled with the kind of joy that surpasses any constraint devised by man or the vagaries of time.

Kelly extended a shaking hand to Clay.

"You're sure?" he asked, still unwilling to claim her unless she voiced her assent one last time.

"I've never been more sure of anything in my entire life."

She uttered the words in such a way that they reminded Clay of a sacred vow. Surging to his feet, he kicked off his moccasins and unfastened his jeans, his heated gaze never leaving her face as he shed his clothing. Straightening, he faced her, basking in the approval he glimpsed in her eyes as she surveyed his nude body.

She confessed, "When I saw you that first time in the shower, I wanted to touch you."

"Then touch me," he invited.

Her gaze dipped and held for several seconds on his engorged maleness and powerful thighs. She hesitated, though.

"You're already touching me with your eyes," he noted, his voice made ragged by the combined forces of desire and restraint. "Do you not wish to use your hands?"

She sucked in a quick breath, then took a step forward.

He took one, as well, effectively closing the distance between them to a matter of inches.

"Closer," he urged, his voice shamanlike in its richness and resonance, even though a firestorm of desire raged uncontrolled within him.

Kelly swayed unsteadily, then asked, "Like this?" when she edged closer.

He nodded, a muscle ticking high in his hard jaw as her orchid scent encompassed him. His eyes skimmed over her face, her shoulders, and finally settled on her breasts. He watched her nipples pucker into tight knots in response to the touch of his gaze.

She widened her stance, but her body continued to sway. "My knees feel like they're about to give way."

Clay drew in a sharp breath, but words proved an impossible feat. His ability to keep his hands off her finally crumbled to dust.

Simultaneously reaching out to each other, their palms met and their fingers tangled. A gentle breeze flowed around them, easing the impact of the midsummer heat but doing little or nothing to quell the invisible flames licking at their souls.

Their palms joined, they inched a little closer, then flowed into each other like dancers performing an erotic ballet. As though Fate had decreed that they would become one, their bodies blended in a lengthy, soul-stirring kiss as they stood breasts to chest and loin to loin.

They sank down upon the blanket a short while later, mouths suddenly ravenous and hands skimming over each other with almost frantic haste as they knelt together.

Time stopped. It lost all meaning, transcended by the eroticism of the moment.

Kelly felt caught up in a maelstrom of sensation from which she knew she would never seek release. Pleasure so complete that it stunned her heart and devastated her senses swept over her like the waves of a heavy tide at the peak of a violent storm.

Clay released her lips and eased her onto her back. She reached for him as he flowed over her and then into the tight channel of her body in a fluid motion that took her breath away.

Settling between her thighs, Clay paused, allowing Kelly the time she needed to adjust to his length and thickness. Her shattered sigh preceded the upward surge of her hips as she took him deeply into her body. Holding her close, he began to rhythmically stroke her with his erection.

Already aroused by what had transpired between them before they discarded their clothing, Kelly felt her insides start to quiver and thrum in response to his movements. She met each and every one of Clay's invasive thrusts with upward tilting motions of her pelvis, the erotic sensations consuming her and sending her over the edge in a matter of a few minutes.

She climaxed with a force unlike anything she'd ever experienced, her body demanding and receiving satisfaction as Clay pushed her higher and harder. She cried out at the pinnacle of her release; Clay's name followed like an incantation, even as he stilled the movement of his hips and held her.

Aftershocks tremored through her from head to toes, and she held tightly to him as the sensations finally began to recede. Gasping for breath and still trembling, she opened her eyes, the shock in them speaking for her as she stared up at him.

"You are perfection," he told her a heartbeat before he took her lips and kissed her with a tenderness at odds with his rugged exterior.

Kelly eventually registered the pulsing strength of his arousal and grasped the extent of his self-control. His leisurely kiss and his seeming reluctance to seek his own satisfaction combined to fan the embers still glowing within her body.

Bringing her knees up on either side of his narrow hips, she rocked against him. Slowly. Deliberately enticing him to join her.

She realized as she watched him lift his head and smile down at her that she loved this man. He would always be a part of her, whether or not he remained a part of her time.

Guided solely by the intensity of the emotions sweeping across her heart, Kelly expressed the depth of her feelings with her body. She

sensed that to speak of love would only burden
Clay, and that was the last thing she wanted to
do.

A second or two later, Clay bit back a groan.
His eyes fell closed. He shuddered, then thrust
deeply into her heat and softness.

"Yes," she whispered against his lips, undulat-
ing beneath him, sucking him into a whirling
vortex of glittering sensation and overt sensuality.
"Oh, yes."

He stopped holding back then, and unleashed
his desire. Guided by primal urges that compelled him to complete this quest for satisfaction,
he accepted her summons and repeatedly
plunged into her steamy, moist depths. He took
her mouth, his tongue matching the rhythm of
his penetrating maleness.

Their pace escalated quickly. His heart
threatened to burst free of his body as they
slammed together. He reached the point of no
return when he felt the spasms taking place deep
within Kelly's body.

His own body responded as she bucked like a
wild thing beneath him. He heard his name on
her lips, knew it signaled that she neared her release. He felt her unravel around his hard flesh,
crying out as another climax seized her and held
her in thrall.

The clutching convulsions of her insides sent
him spinning into the arms of sensory oblivion.
Clay spent himself completely in the moments

that followed, his life-force jetting into her quaking body before he collapsed atop her.

And in the aftermath of such stunning pleasure, he discovered the emotional satisfaction and inner peace he'd searched for his entire life. He found those things, he realized, in the heart and soul and body of a woman called Kelly Jennings Farrell.

NINE

"Michael telephoned while you were in the barn," Kelly said as she took a seat beside Clay on the porch swing the following evening. "I invited him to join us for supper tomorrow night."

Encircling her shoulders with his arm, he tugged her against his hard chest. "Is this a social occasion or another foray on behalf of the Tribal Council?"

"Just friends sharing a meal, that's all. Very relaxed and casual. Black tie not required." Twisting to face him, she studied his profile with the aid of the muted light of the moon. "No hidden agendas allowed on the menu. I took the liberty of warning him."

Clay smiled, clearly amused by her protectiveness. "Thank you, my lioness. If anyone else challenges my wishes, I shall direct them to you."

Kelly laughed. "Any time." She pressed a

light kiss against his chin, then commented in a more serious tone, "It's not his way to badger anyone, Clay, but I suspect he's having a real problem with his promise not to reveal your presence to the council."

"I've told him I have little or nothing to offer my people, especially considering my current circumstances."

"He obviously doesn't agree. You're a gifted man. Michael isn't blind or deaf. Neither am I, for that matter."

"My gift, as you call it, is the unknown. I might disappear next week or next month." He released her, abandoned his seat on the swing, and walked to the porch railing. "It could also happen in the next ten minutes."

"I kind of doubt it," Kelly responded thoughtfully.

She really did doubt that Clay would leave, unless he chose to. Some instinct she couldn't even label assured her he had been delivered to this time in history for an important reason, even if he hadn't yet been able to define it to his own satisfaction.

Kelly pondered him in the semidarkness. Clad in his usual jeans and cotton shirt, and with his nearly waist-length hair streaming down his back, Clay looked primitive and powerful. She knew his power as a man, just as she now knew his skill and tenderness as a lover.

She recalled the heart-stopping pleasure she'd

experienced with him during their afternoon in the pasture and again during the night they'd spent together in her bed. She sighed, her sense of herself as a woman restored and her emotions more vulnerable than ever before. She loved him, and she sensed that she always would, regardless of what happened in the weeks and months ahead.

Although she'd spent the better part of the day telling herself it was enough that she'd discovered her capacity to love again, her heart didn't want to believe such logic. It wanted Clay, just as much as she wanted him.

"What causes your doubt?" Clay asked after several silent minutes.

"Several things," she answered, almost relieved not to have to dwell on the feelings he inspired. "To start with, you speak several languages quite fluently."

"That does not set me apart. I had an excellent education," he reminded her. "Unless the world has gone completely awry, I am confident that many others have had the same advantages I enjoyed."

"I don't know too many people who speak French, Spanish, German, English, and Cheyenne. In fact, I don't know any," Kelly informed him, in spite of the fact that he appeared to be only half-listening to her. She knew otherwise. Clay missed very little.

She continued, undaunted by his dismissive

attitude as she warmed to her subject. "You were quite eloquent this morning in the barn when you shared your childhood memories of the area in and around Sand Creek. I suspect you must have been something of an orator in your world. You're also a Harvard-educated attorney, which is still a very impressive achievement in this country, although you might need a few refresher courses if you decide to take the bar exam and practice law again. And from what you said during supper tonight, I'm certain you're more familiar with the treaties signed in the mid-1800s by the various tribes than any other living person, and I don't think you were at all surprised when I told you they'd all been broken by the same government that drafted them in the first place."

Clay turned, his expression unrevealing as he peered at her. "You're very well informed."

"I pay attention, especially when someone or something is important to me. Now, shall I go on?" Kelly asked.

He inclined his head in that drawing-room way of his.

"You're a real-life historical resource, and you could make a remarkable contribution to the lives of the Cheyenne and their children." Kelly shifted forward, her expression earnest and her tone fervent. "The children are in jeopardy, Clay. Their traditions make no sense to them, and their self-esteem is fragile as they try to navigate between two very distinct worlds. Kids like Joey and his cousins need your influence and guidance. They really do."

"I have no experience with children."

"They're people, Clay. Just very short people with curious minds and great innocence until they start dealing with the world. You don't have to be a rocket scientist to teach them to respect themselves, their heritage, and the world around them. You just have to care about them and their future."

"I am not a scientist. All of nature should be respected as a gift from the Great Spirit. We are the caretakers of our world, and it should not be claimed, or examined under a microscope, or analyzed in a laboratory that stinks of foul-smelling concoctions. I disliked that part of my education," he confessed with a frown, "although I do not remember the study of rockets."

"They came later," she said, determined to keep his attention on the current topic. She decided to save rockets, airplanes, and routinely scheduled NASA trips to the moon for another time. "Whether or not you realize it, you're an instinctive teacher."

"You're wrong."

She pushed to her feet and crossed the porch to stand before him. "No, I'm not wrong. I saw you with Joey, remember? You were patient and attentive with him, and you spoke *to* him. You didn't dismiss him as inconsequential simply because he's a little boy. You treated him with respect. Those are the qualities I look for when I hire a teacher."

"I will need a catalogue for all your moods, won't I?"

Kelly exhaled and told herself to calm down. "Probably. Look, I know I can get a little carried away at times, but I can't always help myself. I just don't think you realize the impact you could have on the Cheyenne people."

"You remind me of someone I once knew," he said after several reflective moments.

"A woman?" Where did that come from? she wondered as jealousy streaked across the landscape of her heart like a star shooting across the heavens.

He nodded. "My mother."

That settled her down in short order. "Is that good?"

Clay smiled. "She was like you in many ways. She went against the guidance of her father and the village elders when she married my stepfather. She cared deeply about him, and she made many sacrifices so they could share their lives. She could be gentle, but she possessed a fierceness of spirit that often shocked those who thought they knew her. I think she enjoyed confounding the wives of my stepfather's colleagues. I suspect it was her personal game, played very much with the approval of a very loving husband." He fell silent for a few moments, then revealed, "She died believing that I would one day liberate the Cheyenne from the repressive laws instituted by the government. Unfortunately, I did not fulfill her dream."

"You had no time," Kelly gently reminded him..

"No." He exhaled, the sound heavy with regret. "No time at all."

"Was your mother happy in her marriage?"

"Very happy." Clay took her hand and tugged her against him. Sliding his arms around her, he held her. "Clayton had lived among the Cheyenne, and his respect for our ways was always evident. You have much in common with my mother. She possessed your honesty and your intensity when she embraced a cause. And she also allowed her heart to guide her much of the time."

Kelly pressed her lips against the side of his neck. He smelled of soap and leather and horses, and she adored the mingling scents as they emanated from his warm skin. She also savored the steely strength of his muscular body. She felt fragile and feminine when he held her close.

"What was your life like in Boston?" she asked, her curiosity about him endless.

He leaned back and peered down at her. "It is a boring tale."

She shook her head. "I won't be bored."

He guided her back to the porch swing. Once they sat down, she leaned back against him, savoring his closeness and the feel of his arms looped around her waist.

"When my stepfather was released from the army, he took us to his family home in Boston. We lived on an estate that overlooked Massachusetts Bay. I'd never seen the ocean before, and I was fascinated by it. Clayton inherited his family's banking business, and he took over the management of the bank shortly after we arrived. He was always very protective of my mother, and he helped her as much as he could as she adjusted to her new life, but it was difficult for her."

"And for you?" Kelly interjected, certain he'd walked a tightrope between the two worlds he'd been forced to inhabit through no fault of his own.

"At times," he conceded. "I was twelve winters when we left Colorado, just entering manhood. I felt compelled to protect my mother, which often put me at odds with the white world. Despite how open-minded people claimed to be, their ignorance and lack of respect often hurt her. This angered me greatly, although she never spoke against these people. She would tell me it didn't matter to her what anyone other than Clayton thought of her. She adopted many of the white ways, even wore the clothing deemed appropriate by my stepfather's sisters when they went out to places like the opera or to dine with others of Boston society, but in private she dressed as a Cheyenne woman, which is how she thought of herself until her death."

"You miss them, don't you?"

"Very much, but at least they were together at the end."

She already knew about the tragic carriage accident that had caused their deaths, so she sidestepped it. "Were you sent away to school?"

"No. Clayton realized it would be best to hire tutors to prepare me for college. He was a good man, and he cared for me as he would have cared about a son of his own blood. He was very patient. I admired him, and I gave him the respect due a father. He seemed to understand that I wouldn't fit in with the sons of his friends. He left many of the decisions about my life in my hands, although this was not the custom among his peers."

"You must have felt isolated and trapped at times," she remarked, saddened by the possibility that he'd been forced to endure so much heartache as a youth.

"Extremely isolated. I had known few restrictions among the Cheyenne. The rules of the white world frustrated me, and I didn't conceal my feelings at first. In truth, I was angry that I had been taken away from all that was familiar to me. I rebelled, but eventually I adjusted to what was expected of me in the ranks of the upper classes. Clayton allowed me as much freedom as possible, the servants indulged me, and my tutors challenged me. I came to enjoy my studies. We also had a full stable, and I rode often."

"What kind of law did you practice?"

Clay chuckled.

She turned in his loose embrace to look at him. "Why are you laughing?"

"Your curiosity has no end."

"Do you mind?" Kelly asked.

"Not at all, but I am also curious."

"About my life? What would you like to know?"

He cupped her face with his hand, leaned down, and took her lips in a searching kiss that scalded her senses. She sank into his passion, surrender as instinctive as breathing whenever Clay touched her or kissed her. She'd never felt more sensory harmony with another person, nor had she ever felt such incendiary desire.

His fingertips drifted down her body. He freed the buttons of her blouse, then slipped his hand beneath the fabric.

Kelly trembled when his hands closed over her high, full breasts. She moaned into his mouth as he caressed her, then shivered delicately as he began to tug at her taut nipples.

Lifting his head several minutes later, he gazed down at her. "I would like to know why you are here for me. It's as though you are a part of some grand design."

With his fingertips still plucking lightly at her nipples, she struggled to respond in a coherent manner, in spite of the tantalizing sensations spiraling through her body. "Not everything can be explained, Clay. Some things . . ." She paused and took a steadying breath, then started again. "Some things, as my very wise grandmother used to say, have to be taken on faith."

He nodded, his expression thoughtful. "I am grateful, nonetheless."

"So am I." Kelly whimpered with delight as he encompassed her breasts with his hands and massaged the swollen globes with his fingers. "When you touch me this way, I can barely think."

"Then do not think," he advised.

He lifted her without warning and brought her to a position atop his thighs so that she faced him. With her knees braced on either side of his narrow hips, she half-knelt astride him, her gently swaying breasts level with his mouth.

She watched in rapt fascination as he captured one of her nipples with his lips and sucked it deeply into his mouth. She felt as though she'd been drawn into a whirlpool of pure sensation from which she didn't want to be rescued.

As he swirled his tongue around the distended tip, he also smoothed aside her blouse. It fell to the floor and was forgotten.

Gripping Clay's shoulders, Kelly curved her upper body over him as he suckled her. Ribbons of heat unfurled throughout her body. Assaulted by emotions and feelings too diverse and far-reaching to describe, she groaned his name and shook with pleasure.

He eventually shifted his attention to her

other breast, tormenting the dark mauve nipple with darting, catlike strokes of his tongue. He used his teeth on her as well, but with great care and precision. His hands remained in motion, smoothing over every curve and hollow of her naked upper body.

"You're very good at this," Kelly said with a gasp when he paused and allowed her to see his face again. "Almost too good."

He considered her remark before responding to it, a hint of a smile lighting his eyes. "A wise man does not discuss the women he has known, and an even wiser woman does not care."

She barely heard his reply, because it suddenly didn't matter who had come before her or the extent of his experience with other women. All that mattered, she realized, was that they were together now.

Kelly reached down between their bodies, her fingertips dancing across the ridge of flesh barely restrained by his clothing. "I want you."

He shuddered, and she finally saw a crack in his famous self-control. "And I want you," he admitted.

"I want you now."

He smiled. "My lioness has become demanding."

Kelly shook her head. "I never demand."

His smile faded. She was right. She simply gave, guided by some instinct he didn't completely understand, but that made her even more precious to him. "Your undemanding nature is one of your most notable attributes."

"I'm glad you approve," she whispered against his lips, her fingers leaving a trail of lightning across his straining groin, up his hard belly, and back and forth across the width of his muscled chest.

"I do approve, more than you will ever know."

She shifted backward a few inches, released the buttons that secured his jeans, and freed the pulsing power of his maleness. Clay jerked as she deftly stroked and teased him until she almost destroyed his control. Spanning her waist with his hands a few minutes later, he effortlessly pushed to his feet and cradled her against his chest.

As he carried her into the house and up the stairs, Kelly knew his destination was the bed they'd shared the previous night. She sighed with relief and looped her arms around his neck. She said nothing, because they clearly wanted the same thing.

Tumbling her back across the wide bed, he stripped what remained of her clothing from her body and then shed his own. When she started to move to the center of the mattress to make room for him, Clay shook his head, caught her by the ankles, and tugged her back toward him. With her legs hanging over the side of the bed, she watched him, eyes wide with uncertainty and breathless with anticipation.

He smoothed her thighs apart once he dropped to his knees at the edge of the bed and bracketed her hips with his hands, but he paused. "Trust me?"

Kelly nodded. "Always."

The smile he gave her before he lowered his head and whispered kisses up the insides of her thighs reached into her soul like a caress.

He left no part of her untouched as he initiated an erotic foray that soon had her gasping for air and quaking atop the mattress. He thoroughly stunned her senses and her heart in the minutes that followed, his open-mouthed kisses to her most delicate flesh, when coupled with the darting and often penetrating strokes of his tongue, more devastating than anything she'd ever experienced with a man.

He took his time with her, as though actually indulging himself as he aroused her to a fever pitch, soothed her until she calmed somewhat, then aroused her yet again. His long hair flowed over her lower abdomen as he made love to her, the silken length tantalizing her already sensitive skin. Reaching down, she caught a few strands between her fingers, then watched with a dreamy expression on her face as the strands drifted down across her thighs.

She began to fear that she might fly into a thousand pieces before he finished with her, but she ceased to care as one wave of sensation after another rolled over her. She quivered in response. She lost touch with everything and everyone but Clay as her insides began to tighten and thrum.

He finally pushed her over the edge with his skillful lips and tongue and hands, the resulting implosion summoning a shocked cry from her as her body trembled with reaction. She thought her climax might go on forever. As she fought for air, Kelly sank back down across the mattress, too drained to do anything but moan softly.

When Clay stretched out beside her and drew her into his arms a few moments later, he noted, "You're purring."

"Mmmmm," she agreed, too weak at that moment to make a speech.

He laughed, hugging her close and giving her the time she needed to reclaim her wits and her emotional balance.

He kissed her a little while later when she opened her eyes and looked up at him. As he kissed her, his tongue probing deeply into her mouth, she tasted her own unique essence and vowed she would know him in the same intimate way.

Gently pushing him onto his back, Kelly knelt beside him and slowly dragged her fingers over the smooth dark skin from his shoulders to his loins. She lingered for a time over the nest of curls that framed his maleness, then skimmed her fingers up and down his engorged shaft. She started to lean forward, intent on giving the pleasure she'd received.

She paused, though, when she felt Clay's restraining hand on her shoulder. She glanced up at him, surprised to see the concerned expression on his face.

"You need not," he told her.

Ever the gentleman, Kelly thought, amazed all over again by his sensitivity to the tolerances of others. "Oh, but I *need* very much," she countered. "I want to taste you."

She saw his shock, felt the pulsating response that added even more strength to the erection clasped between her hands, and sensed that, despite his obvious and probably vast experience with women, he was unprepared to be on the receiving end of this particular brand of intimacy. She was secretly glad, because it made her gift to him that much more unique.

Kelly smiled, a sensual smile worthy of the first Eve, as she recalled what he'd said to her earlier. "Trust me?"

"Always," Clay vowed, repeating the word that she had used as a reply.

Bending over him, she smoothed her hands over his powerful thighs, clasped him once again, then slowly took him into her mouth. She loved him as generously as he had made love to her, her lips and tongue tantalizing and tormenting until a series of long, low groans burst free of him.

His body quaked with the strain she caused, the muscles bunching just beneath the surface of his perspiration-sheened skin. He gripped the bedsheets, his hands fisting in the fabric, his legs shifting restlessly.

Kelly stroked and kissed and licked, then sucked him into her mouth until she felt the press of his hard flesh against the back of her throat. She expressed the depth of her feelings for Clay as she repeatedly drove him to the edge of madness, and each time she sampled his essence. She heard the guttural cry that escaped him just seconds before she felt his hands seize her shoulders.

Clay dragged her up the length of his body. With a hand at the back of her head, he guided her lips to his, fused them, and thrust his tongue into her mouth.

She felt claimed as she crouched over him, and the feeling inspired the need to claim him as her own. Slowly lowering her hips, she impaled herself with his length. She sank down upon him, sheathing him so completely that the distinction between their individual bodies ceased to matter.

Clay surged upward, his hands at her hips as he repeatedly penetrated and withdrew from the wet heat of her body. She matched him thrust for thrust. Their pace quickly grew reckless and abandoned. He rolled her onto her back without releasing her lips or breaking the rhythm they'd created.

Their bodies bonded in the ultimate mating

ritual, they reached release within seconds of each other, their cries mingling in the silence of the Colorado night.

They clung to each other, too stunned and too winded to speak for a very long time. They slept little that night. Insatiable, their desire for each other eclipsed all other considerations.

TEN

Clay was steadily pulling away from her. Kelly knew it as well as she knew her own name. She even understood the cause.

As she walked into the kitchen late the next afternoon, she vowed yet again not to stand in his way. He deserved time to come to terms with the uncertainty he faced without any interference from her.

She also knew she was a complication he didn't need, although she realized now that he wanted her in his life. He'd said as much during the previous long night of sensual indulgence that still had the power to astound her every time she thought about it.

But Clay had also voiced his anxiety that wanting wasn't always enough. Too much had happened to him already, not just the fact that he'd been jerked forward more than a hundred and thirty-five years through some spiritual time warp she didn't even comprehend.

Unprepared for the stunning physical and emotional intensity of their lovemaking, he'd been reflective and withdrawn ever since breakfast, as well as throughout the day as they'd worked in the adjoining corrals with Bountiful and Sinner's Pride.

She loved Clay, very deeply, but he still hadn't determined his place among the Cheyenne, and until he did, neither one of them would know a moment of peace. She muttered a word she rarely used, then told herself to stop acting like some lovesick adolescent.

"That doesn't sound like you at all."

Kelly turned at the sound of Michael's voice. "I know all the bad words. I made a list when I was twelve, much to the chagrin of my mother when I recited it to her over lunch one Saturday afternoon."

He chuckled. "You may remember them all, but you don't use them unless you're really upset about something." Michael crossed the kitchen. "Want to talk about it?"

She shook her head. "No, thank you, *Doctor* White Horse. I don't need counseling at the moment."

"What do you need?"

She said the first thing that popped into her head. "Joey. I miss him . . ." She did need him and miss him, she realized, tears stinging her eyes. ". . . so much."

"He'll be home tomorrow, won't he?"

Kelly smiled for the first time that day. "Thank God for small favors."

He handed her the bottle of wine he'd brought, then dug through a kitchen drawer near the sink for the opener. He behaved with the easy familiarity of an old friend who knew the contents of the kitchen as well as its owner.

"Bingo!" he said, seizing the opener and shoving the drawer closed. "I smell lemon-herb chicken and parmesan noodles, don't I?"

"Your nose still works," she teased.

"Tell that to my sinuses. They've just barely survived the pollen season."

She grinned at him, grateful for his benign conversation. She felt herself starting to relax a little. "I keep telling you to see an allergist."

"The medicine man gave me something."

She arched a brow. "He gives you something every spring, and it never works. You need something stronger."

"Maybe," he said with a shrug. After removing the cork, he set aside the wine so that it could breathe before they sampled it. "I don't want to offend Black Crow. He's a touchy old guy."

"Then don't tell him, just go see a doctor."

"Nag, nag, nag. You sound like my mother."

Kelly laughed. "Thank you. She's a smart

lady. You, on the other hand, are just like the rest of your gender, and that's not a compliment."

He pursed his lips.

She knew he was trying not to laugh at her cranky mood.

"Speaking of my gender, where's Clay?"

Kelly's amusement faded instantly. "He's busy. He'll join us when he's ready." In truth, she didn't know where he was, but she didn't feel like admitting it to Michael.

"You two okay? Things looked pretty harmonious between the two of you the last time I was here."

"Just fine," she said, sounding so terse to herself that she winced. "Sorry. Don't mind me. I'm in an odd mood."

"I meant my promise that I wouldn't say anything to Clay about the council, so you don't have to worry about me committing any major faux pas tonight," he said, his tone emphatic.

"See that you don't. Clay's had a tough time up until now. He needs the space to work through this situation on his own."

"You need not defend me, Kelly," Clay said from his position in the kitchen doorway. "I am more than qualified to mount a defense, in the event that one is even warranted, which it is not."

Startled by his cold tone, she jerked a nod in his direction. "You're right, of course. You don't need help from me or anyone else."

Michael's eyes widened, but to his credit, he

didn't interfere. He didn't even breathe for a long moment as his eyes shifted between the two.

Clay frowned, making no attempt to conceal his disapproval.

Kelly glared at him as she headed in the direction of the living room. "I think I'll get some fresh air."

"She's angry," Clay observed as he strolled the rest of the way into the kitchen.

"Sounded that way to me." His expression neutral, Michael picked up the wine bottle. "How about some Chenin Blanc? It's from one of my favorite California wineries."

Clay nodded, watching as Michael filled two long-stemmed wineglasses with the pale liquid. He indulged his senses by breathing deeply of the fruited essence of the grapes, then sampled the cool liquid. "The French vintners finally have a viable competitor," he remarked.

Michael took a taste of his wine, his pleasure obvious. "For several years now. The American wine industry is now considered one of the finest in the world."

"If this is a sample of their product, I can understand why."

Michael studied him, his expression growing serious. "You seem to be holding your own, all things considered."

Clay smiled, but there was little real amusement in his facial expression. "I'm pacing myself."

"Makes sense," Michael concluded as he settled into a chair at the kitchen table.

Clay took a seat opposite him. "You are remarkably circumspect this evening."

Michael shrugged. "I've been warned. Kelly's very protective of you, so I have to be on my best behavior."

"Kelly is many things," he remarked. "She . . ." Clay hesitated, pondering how to speak of this woman who had captured his heart without revealing the extent of his feelings or the dramatic shift in their relationship in recent days.

"She is a woman of great heart," Michael said.

Startled by the man's choice of words, Clay inclined his head in agreement.

"She's also a very sensitive woman who has been alone for a long time, but you already know that, don't you?"

Clay speared him with a hard look. "Your point?"

"No point, actually," Michael said, stepping back from the subject of his cousin's widow and the mother of his favorite godson.

Clay exhaled, then said quietly, "I have no wish to cause her pain."

Michael's expression unexpectedly hardened. "Then don't. She doesn't deserve that from you, especially not now."

He knows that we are lovers, Clay realized.

The object of discussion chose that moment

to walk back into the kitchen. Under Clay's watchful gaze, Michael got up and filled a wine-glass for his hostess.

After asking Kelly if she needed help serving supper, which she declined, Michael resumed his place at the table. "Did you see the article in the Denver paper about the open hearings the Department of Interior is planning?"

Kelly opened the oven and withdrew a baking dish filled with chicken breasts simmering in a lemon, garlic, herb, and wine marinade. She glanced at Michael. "Not the mineral rights issue again?" she asked, her disgust apparent in her tone and facial expression.

His lioness was in a temper, Clay thought as he watched her place the baking dish on the countertop and cover it with a lid. He didn't comment, however.

"Good guess," Michael answered, sounding grim and looking worried.

"Why is this a problem?" Clay asked.

"The Cheyenne and two other tribes have refused to allow mineral rights exploration on their lands for several years now. The federal government is trying to reverse their stance in the court of public opinion. It's a public relations nightmare for the tribes, especially when the government claims that certain old treaties don't prohibit the exploration they'd like to conduct. The tribes are being cast in a bad light because of their resistance."

Kelly jerked off her oven mitts and slapped them on the counter. "Those bureaucrats don't know when to quit."

"I assume you have legal representation," Clay remarked.

Kelly and Michael glanced at each other, then both looked at Clay.

He saw the speculation in their eyes. "I'm not volunteering for anything. I'm simply curious," he cautioned them.

"We have attorneys in Denver on retainer." As she spoke, Kelly reached for dinner plates from the cupboard and placed them next to the napkins and silverware on the countertop near the covered serving dishes.

Clay noted her use of the word *we*. Her loyalty to the Cheyenne still surprised him, but it also fortified his certainty that she had been selected for him by the Great Spirit. Until he understood his other purpose in this time, however, he hesitated to declare his feelings to her.

Michael leaned forward in his chair. "I've got some of the documentation that's been assembled by our lawyers. Feel like taking a look at some of it when you have a little free time? Your perspective would be quite unique."

Clay was curious in spite of himself. "I will study the documents, but first I must complete two other tasks." He met Kelly's questioning gaze, but only briefly. He focused on Michael

White Horse. "I have decided to accept your guidance and speak privately with the council."

"When?" Michael asked, his shock apparent.

"Tomorrow, if you can arrange the meeting on such short notice."

"Consider it done. We'll have a closed session prior to our regular monthly meeting. What else?" he asked. "Is there anything I can do to help?"

"There is nothing more for now. I must leave here after I speak to the Tribal Council. I don't know how long I'll be absent." Clay didn't allow himself to look at Kelly. He didn't want to see in her green eyes the betrayal she probably felt, so he continued to make eye contact with Michael. "It is time to undertake my quest."

"A vision quest?"

Clay heard the reverence in his voice. He sensed that Michael understood the gravity of the step he was about to take, sensed as well that he knew Clay might not survive the experience. "Yes. A vision quest."

"When did you decide all this?" Kelly asked, her fair skin paler than usual and her fingers white-knuckled as she gripped a full salad bowl.

Clay made himself look at her. "This afternoon. I am physically and mentally able to seek the truth, but the final outcome is in the hands of the Great Spirit." He hesitated when he saw the pain reflected in her eyes, and he silently cursed himself for causing it. It could not be helped or changed, though, and he suspected that she grasped this simple fact as well as he.

After carefully weighing his words, Clay cautioned, "It is possible I will not be guided back to this place or this time, but the risk is necessary. I cannot put it off any longer."

"There is a holy place in the mountains," Michael said, his expression somber.

"Eagle Summit," Clay confirmed, grateful for Michael's presence and intervention—grateful, too, that he was such a staunch friend to Kelly. He feared she might need to depend heavily on Michael if something went wrong during his quest. "I know the place well. It is where I will begin my journey."

Silence descended upon the kitchen for the next several minutes. Kelly was the one who finally ended it. "Our buffet supper is ready, gentlemen. We all obviously need our strength, so let's eat before the food gets cold."

Clay privately applauded her courage and her grit. She was truly a unique creature. She cared for him in her own special ways—in a thousand and one simple, nurturing ways that warmed a man's heart and nourished his soul. In complex sensual ways that evoked explosive passion, the kind of passion he'd always dreamed of but had never experienced with a woman he loved.

He could no longer imagine his life without her. He didn't even want to contemplate the possibility that they might be separated for all eternity. The very thought that he might never see her again filled him with anguish, but his destiny could not be ignored.

Clay glanced at her. The expression on her face assured him that she understood the gravity of the test ahead of him. Although he longed to embrace and comfort her, he sensed that to do so would undermine her emotional balance, which he suspected she was even now struggling to maintain.

"I don't know about you two, but I'm starved," Michael said as he pushed to his feet and walked across the room.

Clay followed him, but instead of taking a plate and serving himself, he paused in front of Kelly. "Trust me."

She lifted her chin, stubbornness visible in her eyes despite the tears also brimming in them. "Always," she whispered. "Always."

Clay nodded, hating the fact that he had to pretend he hadn't fallen in love with her, but for her sake he pretended. He pretended all through dinner. He kept on pretending until he made his way back to the hired man's quarters alone later that night.

Kelly couldn't sleep, so she stopped trying. She left her bed sometime around two in the morning, pausing in front of the window that provided a view of the barn. She briefly debated her limited options, although she knew what she needed to do. It no longer mattered to her that she might be making a total fool of herself by going to Clay. Her heart told her she had no other choice.

She recalled that Clay and Michael had left the house at the same time, eliminating the opportunity for personal conversation. She sensed that Clay had planned it that way. Why, though, she wasn't certain. She needed the answer to that question and others. She needed them now, she realized.

She quietly pushed open the door to the hired man's quarters a few minutes later. She stood in the semi-darkness of the doorway, her nightgown-clad body outlined by the dim hallway light behind her.

"Come in," Clay invited.

Kelly crossed the room, not surprised that he was awake. He required less sleep than most people under normal circumstances, and the circumstances of this particular night were hardly normal.

Pausing at the side of Clay's bed, her gaze swept over him. Her eyes had finally adjusted to the darkness, and she saw he was sitting up in bed, a mound of pillows wedged behind his back. A sheet covered the lower half of his body, but his chest was bare.

"Would you like to sit down?" he asked.

She gratefully sank down onto the edge of the

bed. Shaking and unnerved by the array of emotions and desire spiraling through her, she feared her legs might not support her much longer if she tried to remain on her feet.

"You are still angry?"

His voice sounded so filled with regret that she almost wept. "I was never angry—just confused and hurt that you kept me in the dark about your plans."

"It was not by design. Circumstances conspired against me." He reached out and peeled her fingers from their grip on the edge of the sheet. "Against us."

"Is there an *us*? I thought there was, but now I'm not so sure." Kelly held her breath during the ensuing moments of silence.

His expression troubled, Clay finally admitted, "I don't have the answer to that question."

"Will you ever have the answer?" she asked, half-frightened of his possible response to her question.

He peered back at her in the semidarkness, looking primitive with his long black hair flowing over his nude upper body. She failed to discern his state of mind, because his suddenly enigmatic expression concealed his thoughts and emotions and, once again, gave him the appearance of a living sculpture.

She needed the truth, whatever it happened to be. She also knew she deserved it. It wasn't just her life that would be affected by his choices, but

Joey's as well. For herself and her son she had found the strength to seek answers that others might wish to avoid.

As the seconds passed and began to form minutes, Kelly steeled herself against the reply she expected, her pride asserting itself in the face of Clay's apparent inclination to remain uncommitted. He might have said he wanted her the previous night, but she sensed that those were simply words, perhaps meaningless words, spoken in the throes of passion. She knew that men and women did that sort of thing, but she'd never been guilty of it and couldn't imagine why anyone would want to inflict that kind of thoughtless cruelty on another person.

Unable to stand his silence any longer, she attempted to free her hand, but he refused to release it. "I shouldn't have come to you tonight," she said. "I'm sorry I bothered you."

He exhaled, the sound harsh. "You aren't bothering me."

"But there's obviously no point. You don't have anything to say to me."

He flashed a look of frustration at her. "I won't make promises I might not be able to keep. There is no honor in that kind of behavior. You know that as well as I do, Kelly."

"This isn't about honor, Clay. You have enough of that to take care of the entire planet."

"Now you're angry."

"Aren't I allowed to be?" she demanded. "Is

there some unwritten rule about anger you forgot
to tell me about?"

"I can't make any promises," he insisted
again.

"You're repeating yourself. Besides, life isn't a
bunch of promises that aren't going to be broken.
We're both experienced enough to know that life
is more like a series of opportunities for difficult
choices."

"What choice shall I make with you?"

"You've already made some critical choices
that have had a major impact on me," she reminded him. "You announced them this evening."

"And until I have accomplished those two
things, I cannot and will not compromise you any
more than I already have."

"You haven't compromised me!" she exclaimed. "So get that outdated notion right out
of your head. We became lovers because it was
what we both wanted. You didn't force me or
coerce me. I came to you willingly. That's called
free will, Clay Sloan, and you'd better become
better acquainted with the concept as it applies to
me, because it isn't an exclusively male domain
any longer."

He smiled at her, then brought her hand to
his lips. He kissed her open palm, the tip of his
tongue painting a swath of heat across her skin.

She snatched her hand free and pressed her
palms together, but the scintillating feel of his

openmouthed kiss stayed with her. It also made her a little reckless, and what followed shocked even Kelly.

"I've fallen in love with you, you stubborn man. Deeply in love. Whether or not you come back to me, I will always love you. I trust my instincts where you're concerned, and my instincts tell me with absolute certainty that my future is with you. I don't know if you love me or not. Frankly, I don't feel like I know much of anything at the moment, but I'm trying very hard to be patient, and I'm also trying, obviously without much success, to remain calm."

"Kelly . . . ," he began, alarm in his face as he straightened and reached out for her.

She interrupted him and pushed aside his hands, because she knew if he touched her, her brain would take an extended vacation. "I believe in you, and I believe in what we've shared. That might make me quite provincial in the eyes of some people, but I refuse to apologize for believing real love is the most precious commodity in this world, or in any other world, for that matter."

"I've never known anyone like you," he told her in that low, incredibly seductive voice of his.

Kelly refused to be seduced. "That's wonderfully vague," she snapped. She searched his dark eyes for some sense of how to reach him, and then she remembered something he'd said to her and knew it was important enough to mention now. "While you're out there in the wilderness of Eagle Summit, do something for me, please."

He gave her a curious look. "What?"

"Forgive yourself for all the sins you seem to think you've committed in your old life and in this one. You're a flesh-and-blood man, Clay, not a ghost. Just a flawed human being like the rest of us. You're allowed to make mistakes—it's how we learn important lessons. Like any higher power, the Great Spirit is benevolent enough to value you in spite of your flaws. He does not expect perfection—just a good, solid effort. I believe He's brought you forward in time to be loved and to teach the children of the Cheyenne. If you'll listen when He speaks, I'm convinced that's the message He'll convey to you."

Kelly got to her feet. Clay caught her hand before she could walk away. She met his gaze, certain he was furious with her now.

"You honor me with your love."

"Thank you," she whispered, choking on the emotion swelling in her throat. She swallowed; then, clinging to what remained of her poise, forced herself to speak once more. "I do love you, you know. I love you more than I ever thought myself capable of loving a man. Any man."

Kelly saw the torment in his eyes, saw it clearly in the two tears that hung suspended from his lower lashes. He blinked, and they spilled onto his hard cheeks. They glistened as the moonlight cast a faint glow across his strong features, then finished their journey when they disappeared into the corners of his mouth.

Before she fell completely apart, Kelly fled the room. She departed the barn at a run and kept running as she entered the house and made her way up the stairs to her bedroom.

Her emotions swamped her as she crawled into bed. She cried herself to sleep a little while later, unable to dispel her sense of impending loss.

ELEVEN

Joey arrived home two hours earlier than Kelly had expected, but she knew why the instant he scrambled out of Jenny's van.

"He's fine!" Jenny shouted, referring to the cast on the seven-year-old boy's wrist. "Gotta dash. My three are making me nuts, and I forgot my ear plugs. I'll call you later."

Kelly didn't know whether to laugh or cry as she watched her son drag his heavy duffel bag behind him as he made his way up the path to the front steps of the house.

"What have you done to yourself?" she asked, her gaze on the cast circling his wrist like a bracelet.

Grinning, he released the duffel. "Isn't it neat? I had everyone sign it before we left this morning." He delivered his announcement with obvious pride as he fumbled through his backpack. "I made you a present, Mom, but I gotta find it."

She left the porch, descended the stairs, and paused in front of him. Reassured that all of his other body parts were still operational once she inspected him from head to toe, she noted that his buoyant demeanor was also firmly in place.

Leaning down, she informed him, "The first present I want from you is a hug, young man."

Joey rolled his eyes, but he submitted as his mother drew him into her arms for several lingering moments. "Aw, Mom. How come girls are so into hugging? Melissa Raintree tried to hug me everytime she saw me. It was sickening."

"Melissa has known you since you were a baby. She used to watch you for me before she went away to college." Dropping a kiss atop his head and giving him an extra hug for good measure, she tapped the decorated cast adorning his wrist. "How come no one called me about this?"

"It happened after supper last night. Melissa took me to the 'mergency room. It was too late to call when we got back to camp, but she gave me a note for you." He frowned, resuming his excavation of the carryall in earnest. "It's in here too. I just gotta find it."

"What happened?" she asked.

"I tripped over a log and landed wrong." His eyes got big. "I even heard the bone snap."

"It might be helpful to watch where you're

going," she remarked, trying not to cringe at the bone-snapping comment.

"That's what Melissa said, but I was busy watching a hawk. It was so big, it almost filled the sky, Mom."

Kelly smiled at his awe. She adored seeing him this happy. "Does your wrist hurt?"

"Nah. It did at first, but the doctor gave me a white pill and said it was a . . ."

"Clean break?" she supplied hopefully.

"Yeah. One little bone." He shrugged, then extended a string of beads. "Here's your present. I did it myself. I even made a pattern with the different colored beads. Melissa wanted it, but I told her it was for you."

"I hope she understood." Kelly smiled and then examined the necklace. "It's beautiful. Thanks for thinking of your old mom while you were having fun." She looped the strand of plastic beads around her neck. "How does it look?" she asked.

He inspected her, looking as critical as a ten-year-old could manage to look as he evaluated his handiwork. "Good, Mom. Real good."

"Are you hungry?" she asked. The answer was usually in the affirmative, so she'd baked brownies just after dawn. She hadn't been able to sleep, anyway.

"Nope. Where's Clay?" Joey glanced around, hope and anticipation in his sparkling black eyes. "I really missed him. Aunt Jenny said he likes working here. Is he in the barn? I got a million things to tell him about camp, and I made him a present too. A real leather tobacco pouch. Do you think he'll like it?"

Kelly's smile disappeared. "Joey, why don't we go inside? I need to talk to you."

"He didn't leave, did he? Aw, Mom, please say you didn't send him away?" His face started to crumple.

"Sweetheart . . ." she began, although she was thinking *Damn you, Clay Sloan, you caused this.*

She'd spent the time since abandoning her bed that morning wrestling with how to break the news to Joey that Clay was leaving and might never return. She now regretted even mentioning that he'd stayed on at the ranch during her visit with her son the previous weekend on Parents' Day at Singing Springs Camp.

"Joseph, I would not take my trip without seeing you first."

Kelly flinched at the sound of Clay's voice, then turned to look at him. She reached out to Joey, her hand going to his shoulder, the expression on her face more defensive than she even knew.

Dumping his backpack at Kelly's feet, the little boy shouted, "Clay! I knew you wouldn't go." He launched himself at the tall man, easily slipping free of his mother's restraining hand.

He needs a father, now more than ever, she realized.

Her heart almost shattered as she watched Clay catch him under the arms, lift him high into the air, then swing him around in a circle a few times. The heritage they shared was as obvious as their regard for each other, despite the vast difference in their ages and their limited time together that first day. She'd never seen Joey respond this way to a man—not even to Michael, who was his godfather.

"You are looking well, in spite of your wound. It is not serious, I hope."

Joey shrugged once Clay lowered him to the ground and studied the toes of his shoes. "It's nothin'. I gotta watch where I'm walkin', though."

Clay smiled. He dropped to one knee so that he was at eye level with the boy. "This is a sensible thing to do."

"I made you a present."

Joey the Fearless actually sounded shy, Kelly realized with a pang. She knew why, though, because she knew her son inside and out. He desperately wanted Clay's approval.

She bit back the tears that suddenly threatened as she sank down onto the porch steps and allowed the two of them the privacy of the moment. She would have smiled encouragingly at them if she could have, but her heart ached so badly that she couldn't manage it. She silently reminded herself that neither one of them even seemed aware of her presence at the moment.

"I don't know that I am deserving of such generosity."

"You're my friend, so you are," Joey informed him.

"I'm glad that you think of us as friends."

"I do," he said softly, hero-worship in his eyes as he looked at this man from another time and place. "I had the best time, Clay. I learned about Mother Earth and the Great Spirit. Did you know that horses have souls and that warriors want to be as clever as a fox?" he asked, awe in his voice at the mere possibility that such things were true. "We went fishing and hiking, and I got to be in a secret Cheyenne ritual. I even made friends with a hawk. Maybe next time I go to camp, you could come and visit me with Mom. You could meet my friends, too."

Clay smiled. "I would like that very much."

Kelly listened in shock as Joey seized on Clay's polite response and ran with it. "Then you're not leaving? You're gonna be here and teach me things, and we'll always be friends?"

"That is my hope, Joseph," Clay said, looking alarmed although he kept his voice subdued.

Kelly fought her emotions as she watched her little boy throw his arms around Clay's neck and cling to him.

"You have to stay," Joey pleaded. "It's real important, okay? Cause I don't have my own dad."

"It is important to me as well," he told Joey

once he peeled away the arms locked around his neck and peered into the boy's small face. "I swear to you, Joseph, I will return if it is within my power."

Looking angrier than she'd ever seen him, the boy whirled around and glared at her. "What did you do, Mom? Were you mean to Clay?"

Dismayed by his display of temper, she started to rise from the porch steps, but she paused when Clay lifted his hand to signal that she should wait. Kelly sank back down onto the steps.

"Joseph, I am disappointed," Clay said very quietly as he straightened to his full height.

Joey's chin wobbled. Scrubbing at his eyes with the back of his fists, he looked defeated and suddenly very much like the little boy he was. "So'm I," he announced, still sounding frustrated.

"Shall we walk together, my friend? There are some things I wish to tell you that should only be said to another man." Clay extended his hand and waited.

"Go ahead," Kelly said when Joey looked at her for permission.

She then met Clay's gaze, and she saw—really saw—the anguish and concern for all three of them that was etched into his strong facial features. She could almost feel the pain that emanated from him, and she knew then this man loved her, even if he'd never actually said the words.

She nodded to Clay and watched the two people she loved most in the world as they walked in the direction of the pasture, one little hand tucked in the secure grasp of a much larger one.

Before his voice faded out of range, Kelly heard Clay say, "There is a secret legend I would like to share with you, Joseph, but you must give me your pledge you will never reveal it to anyone."

They were gone for nearly half an hour, but Kelly didn't question either one of them once they returned.

Joey seemed reassured and back in touch with his easygoing personality. Clay also appeared calmer. Belatedly, Kelly realized they had provided each other with a shared experience rare among many fathers and their natural sons.

Michael arrived to take Clay to the Tribal Council meeting just a few minutes after their return. There was no time for lengthy farewells.

Guided by her emotions and instincts, Kelly walked directly into Clay's embrace and stayed there as long as she dared. She derived strength from his touch, and she whispered that she loved him and trusted him. She stepped back, determined not to fall apart as he paused to speak to Joey in Cheyenne.

Her son took her hand as they watched the

two men drive away. "Everything'll be okay, Mom," he said confidently.

Startled, she glanced down at him with amazement. When she asked what Clay had said to him, Joey smiled up at her. "Clay told me he wants to come back to us. I believe him, Mom."

"I'm glad, sweetie. I'm very glad." Kelly summoned what was left of her dwindling emotional strength. "How about a brownie? I baked a fresh batch this morning."

He tugged her up the front path to the porch steps. "Can I have two, and some milk?"

"We'll see," she said. "Let's get your things. I suspect that laundry detail is our first order of business once you unzip that duffel bag."

"Brownies first."

Kelly smiled as they walked into the house. "Only if you tell me more about Singing Springs."

"Sure, Mom." He then launched into a detailed description of the experience.

"I'll check this spot about this time every afternoon," Michael promised several hours later. "If you're not back in a week, then I'm organizing a search party. Agreed?"

Clay nodded, his focus starting to shift inward as he prepared himself for the journey ahead.

Michael placed his hand on Clay's shoulder. "Walk with the Great Spirit, Cloud Dancer, as you seek your destiny." He paused briefly. "And take care of yourself, please, because Kelly will never forgive me if I don't return you to her."

Clay focused on Michael and finally saw the extent of the other man's worry about his welfare. "As a boy I had visions of the future, but I lost that ability when I was taken away from our people. It is my hope that the Great Spirit will see fit to bless me in this way again, so that I will finally understand my destiny. Pray for me, my brother."

"I will pray, and so will the elders who sit on the council," Michael whispered.

"Thank them for me, please, and tell them I hold them in the highest regard. I am strengthened by their confidence in me."

Michael nodded.

Clay turned away from him then and began his ascent to Eagle Summit. He did not look back, nor did he stop climbing until the moon was high in the clear night sky.

He didn't notice the gusting wind, nor did he hear the wailing of the wolves in the distance. He listened to the sound of his own heartbeat. And he prayed.

He prayed to the spirits of his ancestors first, begging them to share their courage with him and guide him in his quest for answers in the great unknown.

He then prayed to the Great Spirit, but rather

than asking for anything, he simply honored the deity he respected most in the world.

Relying on a distant memory from childhood, Clay found a cave just below one of the highest peaks of Eagle Summit. Once inside, he stripped off his clothing, made his way to a stream nourished by the runoff of the late spring snows, and washed himself.

He then traveled even deeper into the cave to a small area once used for purification rites by his shaman grandfather, where he arranged the supplies he would need to cleanse his spirit. The process took three days, during which he fed the fire, sweated the impurities from his body, and emptied his mind of all earthbound concerns. Periodically he drank from the water supply he'd brought, but he allowed himself no food.

He went out into the open on the fourth day. He resumed his trek, this time to the highest peak of Eagle Summit. When he reached the bowl-shaped rock that had been the nesting place of the eagles who had once filled the skies for as far as a warrior could see, Clay presented himself to the Great Spirit.

Although hungry and tired, he displayed his humility, inner strength, and discipline by not demanding or requesting a vision. He simply endured the inclement weather at night, the piercing rays of the sun each day, and the hunger that steadily weakened his body.

Exhausted and almost delirious, Clay finally

felt a strange calm settle over him. He floated with the spirits of his ancestors, who took him outside his mortal body and forward in time. He saw what he was meant to see. He learned of the plans of the Great Spirit. And then he was returned by his ancestors to his unconscious body.

Cloud Dancer, the warrior of the Cheyenne spoken of with reverence among the holy men of his tribe, finally determined his destiny on the seventh morning of his vision quest. Once he regained his awareness of the world around him, Clay made his way down the mountain.

He reflected as he walked. The clarity of his vision astounded him, but he had no doubt that his ability to view the future, and to understand the role he was to play in it, had been restored by the Great Spirit.

He found Michael White Horse in the exact spot he'd last seen him. The stunned look on the man's face prompted him to say, "I am not a ghost, my brother."

"You look like a scarecrow!" Michael exclaimed when he first saw the legend who now walked among The People.

"I'm hungry," Clay conceded, his weathered features showing the strain of the last seven days. "And I would like to go home now."

Joey's godfather beamed. "You had a vision."
"Yes."

"Can you talk about it?" Michael asked as he opened the passenger door of his truck for Clay, then circled around the front of the vehicle and got behind the steering wheel.

"Soon," Clay answered. "For now, though, I must rest while you drive. Are Kelly and Joseph well?"

Michael talked as he started the truck and put it into gear. "She's on edge, and he's as cool as a cucumber. I don't know what you told the boy, but he's expecting you to walk in the door any old time now." Michael laughed aloud when he glanced at Clay, who'd fallen sound asleep.

Kelly gave Clay five minutes to make his way up to the house when she saw him climb out of Michael's truck at dusk. When he didn't, she made certain before she left the house and walked to the barn that Joey was amusing himself with the video she'd rented for him that afternoon.

She found the door to his private quarters open and heard the sound of a running shower. Even though she kept telling herself to take deep breaths and stay calm, she was having trouble following her own instructions. She gave up even trying and raced in the direction of the bathroom.

That door was open as well, and she stepped into the steam-filled room. She waited another full minute. She knew it was a minute because she counted each and every second. The water continued to run.

Kelly finally ran out of patience and pulled open the shower door in the same instant Clay turned off the water. "You've lost weight!" she cried, shocked by the condition of his large body.

Clay scraped his long hair out of his face before he met her alarmed gaze. "I trust that meals are still an aspect of employment I can count on."

"Clay, don't joke. What have you done to yourself?"

"What needed to be done," he said, his voice firm as he accepted the towel she handed to him.

Her tone gentler, she said, "I've been so worried about you."

He smiled as he dried himself. "And now?"

Kelly shot a chagrined look at him. "Now I don't know whether to hug you because I'm relieved you're back or punch you because you haven't taken care of yourself."

"Where is Joseph?" he asked as he knotted the towel low on his hips and stepped out of the shower stall.

"Up at the house."

He advanced on her slowly, one step at a time.

She frowned, but she didn't back up. She couldn't figure out his mood at first.

"Is he occupied?"

She nodded, comprehension dawning even as he reached out for her and began releasing the buttons of the floor-length caftan she wore. "I should caution you, I don't have anything on other than this one item of clothing."

Although he looked ready to drop, he nodded and kept releasing buttons until he'd taken care of all of them. Smoothing the robe off her body, he ran his hands over her like a blind man who required a tactile exploration of those he encountered.

She trembled under his touch, desire flowering deep inside her as she stood before him. His fingers were like little brushes of flame as he skimmed them over her breasts, down across her abdomen, and then into the crease of feminine flesh that quivered the instant he stroked her.

He lifted her into his arms, took her mouth in a deep, probing kiss as he carried her to the bed in the other room, and tumbled her back across the width of the mattress.

"You look so tired," she whispered, her worried gaze traveling over his face as he gathered her close. She brought her hands to his shoulders, so glad to be able to touch him and feel his strength beneath her fingertips that she felt a tidal wave of emotion and relief sweep over her. He was alive, and he was there with her. She cared about nothing else at that moment.

After giving her a lingering kiss, he told her, "I slept on the trip back from Eagle Summit."

"It's probably the only sleep you've gotten since you left here." She knew she was chiding him, but she couldn't help herself.

He inclined his head in acknowledgment of her comment, a tolerant expression on his face as he contemplated her for several moments. Leaning down, he left a trail of flame along the edge of her collarbone with his lips and darting tongue.

"I should probably leave you alone," she said, sounding breathless. It was the last thing she wanted to do.

He lifted his head and gave her a curious look. "Have I not been alone long enough?"

"You're sure you wouldn't rather sleep?"

He settled more heavily between her thighs. "What is your opinion?"

Kelly flushed as she felt the pulsing power of his arousal. She melted inside, her body quivering in anticipation of taking him deeply inside her and holding him there for a very long time. "I guess not," she mused as she released a shaken breath, desire and curiosity mingling inside of her. "I think we should talk a little, though, don't you?"

"There is a lifetime ahead for talking," he told her between nuzzling forays to her neck.

"A lifetime?" Kelly whispered.

"A lifetime."

She shoved at his shoulders.

He looked mildly annoyed. "What is it?"

"Tell me what's going on. I can't stand the suspense any longer. Are you going to be able to stay? Please tell me you aren't going back to your time."

"My future is here with you and Joseph, and among the Cheyenne. I am to be a teacher and advisor."

"You're certain? How can you sound so blasted calm?"

He looked puzzled by her agitation. "Of course. I couldn't be any more certain."

"I've been worried sick about you. And I know I'm repeating myself, so don't bother to tell me, all right?"

Clay rolled onto his side, drawing her along with him so they still faced each other. "Will you marry me?"

She stared at him, not altogether certain she'd heard him correctly. The expectant look on his face assured her she had.

Would she ever not be caught off balance by this man? Would she ever not love him? The answers were as plain as the nose on her face, she reminded herself. She voiced a worrisome thought, the only one that really bothered her. "Am I just another part of your vision?"

Clay shook his head. "You are a choice I make of my own free will, a dream I cannot relinquish, and a need that will never cease." He smiled at her. "Do you require additional reasoning?"

Kelly gave him the answer to his first question. "Yes, I'll marry you."

He laughed then, the sound so rich and free of worry that Kelly couldn't quite believe it was actually coming from Clay. But it was, and she savored it and held it close to her heart. Just as she planned to hold him close to her heart for the rest of her life.

Clay rolled her onto her back. "I've missed you, my lioness. I've discovered I am not complete without you."

"You sound shocked," she said, her fingertips gliding over his cheek.

"I am. I have never loved before."

She saw the truth of his words in his beautiful black eyes and knew she'd never loved him more than at this moment. "You've never said those words to me."

He frowned. "That I love you? I thought you knew."

"I wanted to believe it was possible, but I wasn't sure."

His expression intensely serious, he vowed, "I love you more than life, Kelly Farrell. I will love you for all eternity. You are essential to my happiness and my ability to fulfill my destiny. You always will be."

Tears trailed from her eyes, even though she was smiling. "And I love you."

"I will be a good father to Joseph," he promised.

"And what about our other children?"

Clay looked taken aback. "You are . . ."

She shook her head, delighted she'd rocked his composure a little. He was so self-contained at times that she wanted to shake him. She didn't think he'd lose that quality anytime soon, but knowing she could get a rise out of him every once in a while pleased her.

He tightened his hold on her. "Tell me. Is it not too soon to know?"

"I'm not pregnant yet, but I probably will be soon."

"How can you know this?"

She laughed, thinking of how much he still had to learn about her world. "There are ways to prevent it, and we haven't used any of them."

Clay studied her. "You have taught me to love, but I think you will also teach me how to live."

"Why don't we take one thing at a time?" she suggested.

"I trust your judgment," he told her. "Always."

"And I trust you. Always," Kelly whispered just a heartbeat before he claimed her mouth.

Clay showed her then, in so many delightful ways, just how much he loved her. A little while later, he said, "I need you, my lioness. You have given life to my heart."

He joined their bodies, and they became one. Their hearts, already filled with the joy of their reunion, also became one.

THE EDITORS' CORNER

Spring is just around the bend, and we have four new LOVESWEPTs guaranteed to warm your heart with thoughts of love and romance. Make a new set of friends by reading these touching stories of love discovered, love denied, and love reborn, included in our March lineup. So sit back, relax, grab a LOVESWEPT, and help us usher in a new season of love!

Karen Leabo's *Brides of Destiny* series continues with **LANA'S LAWMAN,** LOVESWEPT #826. Lana Gaston finds she can no longer deny a fortune-teller's prediction when Sloan Bennett appears out of the thunderstorm like a knight in shining armor. She's never forgotten how it feels to lose herself in Sloan's embrace and his steamy kisses. But can a single mom surrender her hard-earned independence long enough to find her future in a street cop's soul?

Karen Leabo maps the territory of true yearning and its power to heal old sorrows in this tale of heartfelt passion and dreams that will never die.

Danger and desire make for a perilous and seductive combination in Janis Reams Hudson's **ONE RAINY NIGHT,** LOVESWEPT #827. Moments after Zane Houston opens his door, shots ring out and he tackles his pretty neighbor, Becca Cameron. Becca is shocked by her reaction to this hard stranger, and when more violence sends them running for cover, attraction gives way to white-hot need. He makes her feel brave and sexy, driving her down a reckless road; but if they survive the ride, will they dare admit it's love? Janis Reams Hudson entangles a desperate ex-cop and a spirited pixie in this story of heartstopping suspense and irresistible passion.

Max Hogan makes a living looking for trouble, but ever since his wife, Grace, sent him packing, he's vowed to find a way back into her life in **EX AND FOREVER,** LOVESWEPT #828, by Linda Warren. Grace insists that she won't be wooed or won over, but when they join forces to catch a clever con man, sparks explode and nothing will put out the flames. He promised her his love for a lifetime. Can Grace convince Max that forever would be even better? Linda Warren's latest story of a couple searching for a second chance is both deliciously sexy and irresistibly funny all at once!

Speaking of second chances, newcomer Stephanie Bancroft weaves a tale of shattering emotion and desperate yearning in **ALMOST A FAMILY,** LOVESWEPT #829. Virginia Catron and Bailey Kallihan had shared the worst that could happen—the loss of their son. Now the child is again theirs to raise. Virginia has struggled past her grief to build a new life, but would rebuilding a family with Bailey mean losing her heart all over again? Stephanie Bancroft poignantly reminds us of how forgiveness can rekindle lost love in this novel of stolen innocence and the power of hope.

Happy reading!

With warmest wishes,

Shauna Summers

Joy Abella

Shauna Summers   Joy Abella

Editor   Administrative Editor

P.S. Watch for these Bantam women's fiction titles coming in March. *New York Times* bestseller Iris Johansen is back with another heartstopping tale of suspense and intrigue. In **LONG AFTER MIDNIGHT**, gifted research scientist Kate Denham mistakenly believes she's finally carved out a secure life for herself and her son, until she is suddenly thrown into a nightmare world where danger is all around and trusting a handsome stranger is the only way to survive. From national bestseller Patricia Potter comes **THE SCOTSMAN WORE SPURS,** a thrilling tale of danger and romance as a Scottish peer and a woman with a mission meet in the unlikeliest place—a cattle drive. And immediately following this page, preview the Bantam women's fiction titles on sale *now*!

For current information on Bantam's women's fiction, visit our new web site, *Isn't It Romantic,* at the following address: **http://www.bdd.com/romance**

GUILTY AS SIN

BY

TAMI HOAG

Don't miss the *New York Times* hardcover bestseller soon to be available in paperback.

The kidnapping of eight-year-old Josh Kirkwood irrevocably altered the small town of Deer Lake, Minnesota. Even after the arrest of a suspect, fear maintains its grip, and questions of innocence and guilt linger. Now, as prosecutor Ellen North prepares to try her toughest case yet, she faces not only a sensation-driven press corps, political maneuvering, and her ex-lover as attorney for the defense, but an unwanted partner: Jay Butler Brooks, bestselling true-crime author and media darling, has been granted total access to the case—and to her. All the while, someone is following Ellen with deadly intent. When a second child is kidnapped while her prime suspect sits in jail, Ellen realizes that the game isn't over, it has just begun again. . . .

"If I were after you for nefarious purposes," he said as he advanced on Ellen, "would I be so careless as to approach you here?"

He pulled a gloved hand from his pocket and gestured gracefully to the parking lot, like a magician drawing attention to his stage.

"If I wanted to harm you," he said, stepping closer, "I would be smart enough to follow you home, find a way to slip into your house or garage, catch you where there would be little chance of witnesses or interference." He let those images take firm root in her mind. "That's what I would do if I were the sort of rascal who preys on women." He smiled again. "Which I am not."

"Who *are* you and what *do* you want?" Ellen demanded, unnerved by the fact that a part of her brain catalogued his manner as charming. No, not charming. Seductive. Disturbing.

"Jay Butler Brooks. I'm a writer—true crime. I can show you my driver's license if you'd like," he offered, but made no move to reach for it, only took another step toward her, never letting her get enough distance between them to diffuse the electric quality of the tension.

"I'd like for you to back off," Ellen said. She started to hold up a hand, a gesture meant to stop him in his tracks—or a foolish invitation for him to grab hold of her arm. Pulling the gesture back, she hefted her briefcase in her right hand, weighing its potential as a weapon or a shield. "If you think I'm getting close enough to you to look at a DMV photo, you must be out of your mind."

"Well, I have been so accused once or twice, but it never did stick. Now my Uncle Hooter, he's a different story. I could tell you some tales about him. Over dinner, perhaps?"

"Perhaps not."

He gave her a crestfallen look that was ruined by the sense that he was more amused than affronted. "After I waited for you out here in the cold?"

"After you stalked me and skulked around in the shadows?" she corrected him, moving another step backward. "After you've done your best to frighten me?"

"I frighten you, Ms. North? You don't strike me as the sort of woman who would be easily frightened. That's certainly not the impression you gave at the press conference."

"I thought you said you aren't a reporter."

"No one at the courthouse ever asked," he confessed. "They assumed the same way you assumed. Forgive my pointing it out at this particular moment, but assumptions can be very dangerous things. Your boss needs to have a word with someone about security. This is a highly volatile case you've got here. Anything might happen. The possibilities are virtually endless. I'd be happy to discuss them with you. Over drinks," he suggested. "You look like you could do with one."

"If you want to see me, call my office."

"Oh, I want to see you, Ms. North," he murmured, his voice an almost tangible caress. "I'm not big on appointments, though. Preparation time eliminates spontaneity."

"That's the whole point."

"I prefer to catch people . . . off balance," He admitted. "They reveal more of their true selves."

"I have no intention of revealing anything to you." She stopped her retreat as a group of people emerged from the main doors of City Center. "I should have you arrested."

He arched a brow. "On what charge, Ms. North? Attempting to hold a conversation? Surely y'all are not so inhospitable as your weather here in Minnesota, are you?"

She gave him no answer. The voices of the people who had come out of the building rose and fell, only the odd word breaking clear as they made their way down the sidewalk. She turned and fell into step with the others as they passed.

Jay watched her walk away, head up, chin out, once again projecting an image of cool control. She didn't like being caught off guard. He would have bet money she was a list maker, a rule follower, the kind of woman who dotted all her *i*'s and crossed all her *t*'s, then double-checked them for good measure. She liked boundaries. She like control. She had no intention of revealing anything to him.

"But you already have, Ms. Ellen North," he said, hunching up his shoulders as the wind bit a little harder and spat a sweep of fine white snow across the parking lot. "You already have."

THE DIAMOND SLIPPER

BY

JANE FEATHER

What comes to mind when you think of a diamond slipper? Cinderella, perhaps?

That's what Cordelia Brandenburg imagines when her godparents arrange a marriage for her with a man she's never met—a marriage that will take her to Versailles, far from her childhood home. The betrothal gift is a charm bracelet with a tiny diamond slipper attached . . . as befits a journey into a fairy-tale future. But when her escort to the wedding is the sensual, teasing Viscount Leo Kierston, it's love at first sight for the young, headstrong Cordelia. And while Leo sees only a spoiled child, Cordelia is determined to show him the woman underneath. But there is no escaping her arranged marriage, and she's devastated to discover that her husband is a loathsome tyrant who will stop at nothing to satisfy his twisted desires. But he also has a terrible secret . . . a secret that will bring a long-awaited chance for revenge, the dark threat of danger, and the freedom of a vibrant passion.

"Which hand do you choose, my lord?"

It seemed that short of bodily removing her, he was destined to play chess with her. Harmless enough, surely? Resigned, he tapped her closed right hand.

"You drew black!" she declared with a note of triumph that he recognized from the afternoon's dicing. "That means I have the first move." She turned the chess table so that the white pieces were in front of her and moved pawn to king four. Then sat back, regarding him expectantly.

"Unusual move," he commented ironically, playing the countermove.

"I like to play safe openings," she confided, bringing out her queen's pawn. "Then when the board opens up, I can become unconventional."

"Good God! You mean there's one activity you actually choose to play by the book! You astound me, Cordelia!"

Cordelia merely grinned and brought out her queen's knight in response to his pawn challenge.

They played in silence and Leo was sufficiently absorbed in the game to be able to close his mind to her scantily clad presence across from him. She played a good game but he had the edge, mainly because she took risks with a degree of abandon.

Cordelia frowned over the board, chewing her bottom lip. Her last gamble had been a mistake and she could see serious danger in the next several moves if she didn't move her queen out of harm's way. If only she could intercept with a pawn, but none of her pawns were in the proper position, unless . . .

"What was that noise?"

"What noise?" Leo looked up, startled at the sound of her voice breaking the long silence.

"Over there. In the corner. A sort of scrabbling." She gestured to the far corner of the room. Leo turned to look. When he looked back at the board, her pawn had been neatly diverted and now protected her queen.

Leo didn't notice immediately. "Probably a mouse," he said. "The woodwork's alive with them."

"I hope it's not a rat," she said with an exaggerated shiver and conspicuously united her rooks. "Let's see if that will help."

It was Leo's turn to frown now. Something had changed on the board in front of him. It didn't look the way he remembered it, but he couldn't see . . . and then he did.

Slowly, he reached out and picked up the deviated pawn. He raised his eyes and looked across at her. Cordelia was flushing, so transparently guilty he wanted to laugh again.

"If you must cheat, why don't you do it properly," he said conversationally, returning the pawn to its original position. "You insult my intelligence to imagine that I wouldn't notice. Do you think I'm blind?"

Cordelia shook her head, her cheeks still pink. "It's not really possible to cheat at chess, but I do so hate to lose. I can't seem to help it."

"Well, I have news for you. You are going to learn to help it." He replaced her rooks in their previous position. "We are going to play this game to the bitter end and you are going to lose it. It's your move, and as I see it, you can't help but sacrifice your queen."

Cordelia stared furiously at the pieces. She couldn't bring herself to make the only move she had, the one that would mean surrendering her queen. Without it she would be helpless; besides it was a symbolic piece. She would be acknowledging she'd lost once she gave it up. "Oh, very well," she said crossly. "I suppose you win. There's no need to play further."

Leo shook his head. He could read her thoughts

as if they were written in black ink. Cordelia was the worst kind of loser. She couldn't bear to play to a loss. "There's every need. Now make your move."

Her hand moved to take the queen and then she withdrew it. "But there's no point."

"The point, my dear Cordelia, is that you are going to play this game to its conclusion. Right up to the moment when you topple your king and acknowledge defeat. Now *move*."

"Oh, very well." She shot out her hand, half rising on her stool, leaning over the board as if it took her whole body to move the small wooden carving. Her knees caught the edge of the table, toppling it, and the entire game disintegrated, half the pieces tumbling to the carpet. "Oh, what a nuisance!" Hastily, she steadied the rocking table.

"Why, of all the graceless, brattish, mean-spirited things to do!" Leo, furious, leaped up. Leaning over the destroyed board, he grabbed her shoulders, half shaking, half hauling her toward him.

"But I didn't to it on purpose!" Cordelia exclaimed. "Indeed, I didn't. It was an accident."

"You expect me to believe that?" He jerked her hard toward him, unsure what he intended doing with her but for the moment lost in disappointed anger that she could do something so malicious and childish. He moved his grip to her upper arms, half lifting her over the board, Cordelia's protestations of innocence growing ever more vociferous.

Then matters became very confused. He was shaking her, she was yelling, his mouth was on hers. Her yells ceased. His hands were hard on her arms and her body was pressed against his. . . .

From the fresh, new voice of

MICHELLE MARTIN

comes a sparkling romance
in the bestselling tradition of
Jayne Ann Krentz

STOLEN HEARTS

An ex–jewel thief pulls the con of her life, but one
man is determined to catch her—and never
let her get away.

*For Tess Alcott, chocolate was a vice, stealing jewels was
pure pleasure. So when her ruthless former "employer"
turned up to coerce her into taking part in a daring heist,
he didn't have to twist her arm too far. He only had to hold
out the lure of the magnificent Farleigh emeralds. To win
them, all Tess needs to do is convince one sweet old lady and
one grouchy, blue-blooded—and distractingly handsome—
lawyer that she's the missing heiress to a fortune. But Tess
doesn't realize the danger, until the infuriating lawyer
beats her at her own game and steals her most prized
possession . . . her heart. Now Tess doesn't know which
she wants more: the gorgeous emeralds or the gorgeous
emerald-eyed lawyer. . . .*

She padded down the back stairs in her bare feet, to
avoid Jane and Luke, and walked into the library.
Luke stood at the river-rock fireplace, a snifter of

brandy balanced in his long fingers. He stared into it as if seeking the answers to the universe.

"Oops! Sorry," she said, striding briskly into the room as if her very being was not centered on the green-eyed monster from hell. "I didn't mean to disturb you. I just came for a book. Something like Richardson's *Pamela*. Guaranteed to knock you out cold inside of two minutes."

"You're looking for *Pamela*?" he said, his hands still wrapped around the brandy snifter. "You nearly fell asleep over your cup of after-dinner hot chocolate."

She walked toward the bookshelves, hoping to find a book and escape quickly. "Hodgkins laced the hot chocolate with caffeine," she said calmly. "I'm convinced of it."

"His dislike of heartless cons exceeds even my own. But then, he's known Jane longer."

"Fortunately," Tess said lightly, "Jane relies on her own opinion, not on that of her butler or watchdog, I mean lawyer."

"This *watchdog* will protect Jane from your machinations with the last breath in his body."

"I expected nothing less," Tess said, scanning the shelves for *Pamela*.

"Who are you really, Tess Alcott?"

"You got me. I'll let you know when I find out."

"So you intend to play this amnesia story for all it's worth?"

Rage erupted in Tess and spun her around to face her enemy. "Do you remember your fifth-birthday party?" she demanded.

Luke looked surprised at suddenly being under attack. "Sure."

"Do you remember what your childhood bedroom looked like?"

"Of course."

"Do you remember what your favorite food was?"

"Yes."

"Well, I don't!" Tess said bitterly. "You're supposed to be such a hotshot lawyer, Mansfield, but you're batting less than a hundred when it comes to knowing what the truth is about me!"

She spun back to the bookshelves, trying to get her temper and her pain under control. The library was silent for what seemed a very long moment.

"I'm beginning to think you're right," Luke said gently. "But still, even with my lousy batting average, you can't win."

"There's that male arrogance rearing its ugly head again," Tess said, standing on tiptoe to read the titles on the upper shelves, wanting to relax into Luke's quiet but not daring to. "But in a way you're right, Mansfield. I can't really win because I don't have anything to lose. I'm looking for my past, remember? If Jane isn't there, it's no skin off my nose. I'll eventually find someone who was there and I'll be able to conduct my own little 'Up Close and Personal' interview. So yap away, Mansfield, you can only give yourself a sore throat."

His chuckle rumbled up and down her spine. Without looking, she knew that Luke had leaned his back against the fireplace mantel and was studying her from head to toe.

"Love your negligee," he said.

Tess forced herself to laugh as she grabbed *Pamela* and turned to him. The brandy snifter was resting on the mantel. His hands were free. He seemed more dangerous that way. "I think it's best to choose function over form," she said a little breathlessly, tension coiling within her. "In my line of work, it's often necessary to make a quick, and unscheduled, exit and that means no time to grab your clothes if you're sleeping in the nude . . . as I found out the hard way in my youth."

Luke's grin broadened, lightening his face, eroding the cynical mask. "Now that is something I dearly would have loved to see."

"Six French *gendarmes* had the dubious pleasure instead," Tess said, walking back across the room. It seemed to stretch on for miles before her. "Fortunately, the shock of seeing a naked girl running across the rooftops of the Left Bank kept them from firing their guns and I was able to make my getaway unscathed. Later I heard about an American bank robber who pulled all of his jobs in the nude because, I am told on the greatest authority, if you've only seen someone naked, you can't recognize them dressed."

"That wouldn't work where you're concerned," Luke murmured, his gaze forcing her to a stop directly in front of him. "It's a good thing you didn't meet those *gendarmes* the next day."

A blush flooded Tess's cheeks. "Why, Mr. Mansfield, I do believe you're actually paying me a compliment."

"It has been known to happen," Luke said, sounding a bit surprised himself. "I once made some very nice remarks about a racing skiff I was assigned at Harvard."

"Careful, Mansfield. Such unbridled enthusiasm will have you running amok."

"Running amok sounds wonderful just now," Luke said with a sigh, his hand reaching out and brushing against her cheek, lingering there, stilling her breath.

The world tilted crazily beneath Tess's feet as he slowly lowered his head to hers. "Luke," she whispered, and had no idea what to say next.

His lips met hers in a gentle joining of warmth against warmth. Hunger broke free within her. She wrapped her arms around his neck, standing on tiptoe to press herself against him, her mouth deepening the kiss of its own accord. With a groan, Luke slid his arms around her, holding her tight, his sensual mouth moving hungrily over hers.

It was good, so good. It was the closest thing to heaven Tess had ever known.

And it ended in the next moment, as sanity abruptly returned.

She jerked away, her book clutched to her chest, the back of one hand pressed against her mouth. "What the *hell* do you think you're doing?" she hissed.

His breath as ragged as her own, Luke stared down at her. Then anger blazed in his eyes. "The same might be asked of you, *Elizabeth*," he said. "Just how far were you willing to go to win me over to your side?"

Something in Tess, newly born, died in that moment. Oh God, he had been using her, testing her. And she had fallen for it. For a moment her hand itched to strike the superiority from Luke's handsome face. Instead, she gripped her book even harder.

"Don't think you can use your masculine charms to seduce me out of this house," she snapped. "I am neither that stupid nor that desperate!"

She stalked from the room, slamming the library door shut behind her.